Ketsanis

A Ghost Story From the Adirondack Mountains

Michael A. M. Coleman

ISBN: 061575032X
ISBN-13: 978-0615750323 (Telotropics Press)

Cover photo Michael Coleman

DEDICATION

For all those who delight in the strange and wonderful,
whether they find it in the crystalline beauty of physical law,
the direct emotion of a simple song,
or the world-transcendent sparkle in a laughing child's eye.

CONTENTS

1 The Blind Ghost of Bunk Thirteen 1

2 The Cleansing of Ketsanis 29

1 THE BLIND GHOST OF BUNK THIRTEEN

CAMP KETSANIS

All camps have their ghost stories: tales best told around a campfire, to friends half-lit against surrounding darkness, from which the eyes of uninvited things may, unobserved, be all-observing – patient, predatory, implacable – awaiting the dimming of the fire and the uncontested dominance of night. Yes, all camps have their ghost stories, and I have been chilled by as many as I suppose, over the years, have you. But only once, for me, has such a story drawn reality into itself and taken me to the place from which all such stories must, I think, first come. So, now: turn down your lights, and let me tell it to you. Listen, if you will, for stirrings in what *ought* to be silence – look, if you must, for any shape of deeper shadow *implied* in the darkness beside you – but attend, if you would learn how deeply strange is this our world, to my tale of Camp Ketsanis and the Blind Ghost of Bunk Thirteen.

Camp Ketsanis was, when I worked there as a counselor in the summer of 1979, a camp for "emotionally disturbed" children on the shore of Lake Ohneka, an hour's walk from the town and station of Lake Ohneka, in the Adirondack mountains well northwest of Saratoga toward Newcomb in New York. The guiding principle of the camp was that an active summer of outdoor sports and Spartan bunk-living was just the sort of unsentimental healthful intervention that emotionally troubled kids could benefit from; the passive ones, like their first-year counselors, would have to come out from their shells to hike and swim and compete with one another, while the aggressive ones under the leadership of tested camp veterans would learn teamwork and find outlets for their energy other than doing damage to their neighbors and themselves.

The camp was laid out as a beach, boathouse, and playing fields nestled between two hills. On one hill, strung along a camp path that had once been a logging road and before that a Mohawk trail into the tall mountains beyond -- Tahawus the cloud-splitter with its neighboring peaks -- stood thirteen bunks and the charred stone circles of our fire-rings. On the slope of the opposing hill stood the *Great Camphouse*, where camp administration resided and in the *Great Hall* of which we took our meals.

The camp property had eighty years before been the family compound of Sigur Sigursson, a Kodak executive nicknamed "Brownie" after the camera he helped bring to market. It was his wife Eva who had given their family compound its name, "Ketsanis," soon after Brownie's sudden death in 1905 from a heart attack while clearing brush beside a disused well-house on the old logging road. She claimed the name was spoken to her out of the darkness on the night of her husband's death, and until her own death 24 years later she maintained that this naming of her family's mountain camp was at the request of "the land itself, which speaks to me in my husband's voice, and is not ours." Fortunately for Eva, a thin veneer of sanity was sufficient to be considered 'eccentric' rather than 'mad' – this was and remains one of the privileges of wealth.

An image from its past presided over the camp as I knew it in 1979. Above the Great Fireplace of the Great Hall of the Great Camphouse hung a double-portrait, by Sargent, of Brownie and Eva's twin daughters, Katrin and Bryndis. Preserved forever as they were in 1906, they were both Burne-Jones beauties of eighteen captured in the dress of Gibson Girls, echoes of one another in figure and face save that the gentle blue beauty of Bryndis's eyes was challenged and upstaged by the pure Icelandic green of Katrin's.

I believe every young man, counselor as well as camper, who has passed through Ketsanis has at some quiet moment paused to look deep into Katrin's provoking green eyes and found himself disturbed by an unattainable desire. Her impact was no less disturbing in her own day: Katrin was said to have scandalously vanished in 1907 when returning by train to Radcliffe for her sophomore year, on the same day a music instructor then boarding with the family had stolen some jewels as dowry and also vanished. Neither had ever been seen again; only this image of Katrin survived her strange elopement, an object of youth and beauty preserved in unchanging perfection through a vanished lifetime of years.

From gentler Bryndis had descended, in the second generation of later Brynns and Katies, one Bryndis Astor Morgan, the present owner of the camp, and her daughter, another Katie of nineteen with the pure blue eyes of great-grandmother Bryndis. Katie Morgan was of around the same age as we counselors, but she usually kept to herself in the family part of the Great Camphouse — a beautiful rich girl's snobbery, perhaps, or a strange one's shyness. It was her mother Bryndis and father Matt (or "Manly" to his counselor-troops, surely with his silent consent) who had made over their estate into a summer camp for emotionally disturbed children; this had been done in response to the suicide of a near relation, Katie Eastman, a diagnosed schizophrenic, who ended her life at nineteen. Manly Morgan was the camp director and promulgator of a philosophy that the emotional turmoil of adolescence is a sort of indulged malingering for which hard work — or, failing that, an unpampered summer of hard play in the mountains -- is a sound corrective, if applied before things get too far out of hand.

When I arrived at Camp I was assigned to be one of two volunteer counselors living and working with the eight passive children of Bunk Four. The first six bunks, closest to the lake along the old camp path, were for the passive kids. Further uphill — quite intentionally, in order to consume more of their troublesome energies -- were the six bunks of the aggressive kids. Beyond them lay bunk thirteen and the most remote of the camp's fire-rings, and after that stretched the endless forest. The most distant bunk, bunk thirteen, was used for storage. It had been used as a bunk for only part of one summer, when all thirteen bunks were newly built and the camp was first opened in 1970.

From the opening of camp that first year, counselors as well as campers were filled with stories that the brand new Bunk Thirteen, built where once that old well-house which pre-dated the Sigurssons had collapsed in decay, was somehow already haunted. On the first night of camp, one terrified camper reported a "blind ghost with no eyes" which clawed at its own face until it became "a bloody screaming skull." The next night several of the other campers said they had seen the blind ghost too, though they all seemed far more excited than terrified. This sort of report from a group of emotionally disturbed children up from the City and bunked out in the night of the Great Northern Woods for the first time in their lives was not calculated to have much impact on Manly Morgan, and within the week all campers had been appropriately intimidated and all reports of blind ghosts, screaming skulls and suchlike panels from horror comics had ceased.

And yet, and yet … other more subtle oddities that were told of by the counselors themselves had *not* ceased. Soft grating sounds were reported, and not only by night, beneath the floorboards – and it seemed the bunk would grow unusually cold when such sounds were heard. When coming back to bunk in the evening, campers' belongings were sometimes found to have been re-arranged – or new objects would be found that no one recalled having seen before. Although none of the doors to any of the thirteen cabins had locks – the temptations permitted by privacy were *not* encouraged by Manly at his camp – only at bunk thirteen would the door be found open to the breezes of the woods every morning. Early risers reported seeing the face and paws of a fox just outside a bunk window, as though foxes could just hover in the air. Once, it was the chilly beauty of green-eyed Katrin "just like in the painting" who was reported visible through the open door at the edge of the woods – a sighting which invited laughing offers of bunk-swaps by other counselors who claimed to have no problem at all with being haunted by pretty Kate.

All these things became the fodder of campfire stories that first year of the camp and ever afterward. None of them, apparently, disturbed Manly Morgan, who threatened that he would reassign the nervous counselors of Bunk Thirteen to one of the "lower six" bunks – and as campers, not as counselors. But four weeks into the summer, a Bunk Thirteen camper was found dead one morning, apparently the victim of sudden heart failure in the night. This was the sort of thing that could get a camp closed down, and after the withdrawal of some campers by their parents the survivors of Bunk Thirteen were reassigned to other bunks, and Bunk Thirteen became a storage shed – and a legend. It was never used as a bunk again.

AROUND THE CAMPFIRE TOGETHER

As a "lower six" counselor, I was understood to be a newbie in need of indoctrination in camp philosophy and camp tradition. I and the other counselor responsible for bunk four, Barry Gadole, known to all as "Bummer" because of a tic of speech, were taken in hand by Chris Hicey ("like high c"), a Harvard guy up at bunk twelve who had been a counselor here for two previous summers and planned to be a clinical psychologist. He had snapped pictures of all the newbies with his Polaroid and posted them on the boathouse wall in tiers whose ranking indicated whether the upper six counselors thought we were earning our keep or failing. Among the girls, alone at the top of the heap was fail-free Astrid Arnheim, a newbie like me, but a triathlon athlete who already had even the upper six counselors following after her. Astrid had been chosen by Chris's summer-girlfriend Karen as protégé, and she already seemed to know years of camp-stories. Chris and Karen, by the way, were in other relationships when not at camp; they understood they would be together only for the summers, and what happened at camp stayed at camp.

Much of my introduction to camp lore took place around a campfire. The fire-ring just above bunk thirteen was a favorite of off-duty counselors after their charges had been put to bed, because it was the most distant and would not disturb the kids. It was perfect for ghost stories. The branches overhead brushed against each other like a rattling of bones, and the darkness of bunk thirteen just below the fire-ring helped any teller of tales exceed his or her skill by lending its ominous malevolence to the storytelling.

One night about three weeks into the summer I joined the usual suspects around the campfire. On walking up the path, I had noticed that the door to bunk thirteen was standing open to the forest night. The door had been found open just that morning, its padlock gone. Manly had been curiously silent about this possible act of vandalism against camp property – perhaps he was used to it, as it happened every summer and had become something of a camp tradition. Chris was telling the strange story of the day: at dinner a camper had come upon Katie Morgan and told her that she "looked like the girls in the picture" and Katie had responded "sometimes I *am* the girl in the picture – and that is a terrible thing to be".

"Great line to give an already-disturbed kid," said Chris. "She's going to wind up as crazy as those other crazy Katies, who both killed themselves."

"I thought Katrin eloped?" I asked. "She didn't kill herself."

"No, but two other Katies did. One was her sister's daughter, Mrs. Morgan's mom. She left a note that read 'let there be an end to Katie' and blew her brains out. And then Katie Eastman, their cousin, only a few years ago — and while she was staying at the camphouse here -- she took her great-aunt's suicide note out of some family Bible and signed her own name below the original signature, then swallowed all the pills in the house."

"At least when these people go crazy," smirked Karen, "they do it with style."

"I suppose the Great Camphouse must be as haunted, then, as bunk thirteen," offered Jenna from bunk two.

Chris grinned at her. "You wouldn't say that if you knew anything about bunk thirteen."

"I've been told about it," said Jenna. "That dead kid – the one with a heart attack. Almost got the camp closed down the year it opened."

"Hell, that's nothing," laughed Chris. "I run bunk twelve – do you know the weird-ass shit I hear from my invisible neighbors next door every night? I tell my kids it's squirrels. Squirrels! I wouldn't go in there if you paid me."

"I would," interposed Astrid, and all eyes turned to her. "I'd go in there. I don't believe in God, or ghosts, or anything at all after death. If that place really is haunted, if I could really believe that, it would change my life."

"You wouldn't last five minutes alone in there," said Karen.

Astrid grinned at her a big healthy grin. "Come with me!"

"Like Hell!" said Chris and Karen in one voice together.

Then I jumped in. "I'll go," I said, and all eyes now turned to *me* in amazement. You see, I didn't give a damn whether we saw a ghost or not, but I had found a chance to be brave in front of Astrid – and to be alone with her.

"Good luck to you both!" spat Chris. "Here comes the next dead-counselor story in the making."

So then there was no choice. Astrid and I stood and looked below us at Bunk thirteen, set in the darkness as a greater darkness, silent and innocent as a trap. We were probably both a little less brave now, but what could we do? We went down to the bunk together, making stupid jokes I've since forgotten.

When we got there the door was open. I went in first. It was like every other bunk – a window on either side of the door, two more on the far side, bunk beds and dressers for two counselors and eight children. There were various crates stacked about, but the beds were free and clear. We sat down and let our eyes adjust to the darkness. I wasn't thinking much about ghosts. I was thinking: Would Astrid let me kiss her?

"Where are the cobwebs?" asked Astrid.

"What?"

"Where are the spider webs? Where is the dust? No one uses this place. Why is it so clean it could pass one of Manly's inspections?"

Astrid was right. This was strange. "Probably because this place is so haunted even the spiders avoid it!" I joked.

"Or because its haunting is so famous that everybody is always daring everybody else to come in here, and the place is as busy as Times Square," laughed Astrid. Then we were silent.

It would have been better if we had kept joking.

When we were quiet, we became aware that the silence and the darkness were *absolute*. The fire-ring was just up the hill – where were the voices? Where was the flicker of firelight? It was as if there were nothing at all outside the open door of the cabin but a black and soundless void. Astrid stood up. Shortly after, I did too. I was no longer thinking about kissing.

And then – I heard a quiet voice in the darkness say: "take us from the well." The voice was perfectly normal, but it had no right being there – unless Astrid and I had been set up for a prank.

"Did you hear that?" I asked, suspecting we were being tricked yet nonetheless moving toward the door, although for a moment I almost imagined a dark form appear and then vanish there. But cool Astrid said, in the dark behind me, "Don't go – this is what we came for! I mean – this is our chance to really know if ghosts are real, if we *just don't run*."

I stopped – I was not going to be the scared one if Astrid had somehow kept her courage. I felt her presence grow close right behind me – if I turned *right now* I would be an inch's distance from a first kiss ... but even as I thought this I heard a distant-sounding voice outside the bunk: "Mike! I heard that! That *isn't me*! I ran for it,

I'm out here," and in a sudden nausea of terror and confusion I fled, spinning when I got out the door and batting at air, like a man who had walked through a massive cobweb, lest some trace of whatever had stood behind me still hung in the air.

We were mocked upon our quick, excited return: "So now bunk thirteen's not haunted by a blind ghost anymore, it's haunted by Astrid!"

The next day, Chris had lowered my Polaroid in the boathouse by a rung. "If any of the rest of us were alone with Astrid in that bunk, my friend," he said, "we would *not* have rushed out like a scared camper – *whatever* else was in there."

KATIE'S STORY

Three nights later, all eight of my kids seemed to be overcome by anxieties and bedtime-fears at once, as if they sensed some pending threat or crisis gathering itself in the night, but after we finally got them all settled into bed and Bummer was comfortably in control, I headed to the upper fire-ring where I hoped to meet Astrid. She had let me kiss her in the boathouse the day before; I hoped that tonight we might take a walk into the woods together, and just kissing would not be the end of it.

Despite the ordeal of settling down the kids it was not *very* late, but the sky was overcast and already perfectly dark, without moon or stars. Bunk thirteen waited ominously beside my path, its door open to the darkness, but as I passed watchfully beside it on my way up to the fire-ring I must confess my mind was running much more on Astrid than on ghosts, and I felt no threat. There was a small fire already burning in the fire-ring, but to my surprise none of the other counselors were there. Perhaps many of their campers were also pulling a night of upsets? I saw Chris's backpack beside a log, with his Polaroid camera and a bottle of water taken out – he must have come up here and lit the fire, but then gone off into the woods with Karen. I would have to give him a hard time, as he would do to anyone else who left a fire unwatched, however small it was. So, I sat down on the log beside his backpack, and waited.

I do not know how long I waited – not very long I suppose, though it felt longer. After a while I got that classic feeling of "you are not alone", and started looking about me more carefully. In the darkness at the edge of the woods I could make out a deeper darkness of roughly human shape. Could it be Chris or Karen coming back to the campfire? No, whatever this was just stood there: patient, immobile. Could it be Astrid up to some prank, trying to scare me? Possibly – and at that point I reached down to Chris's backpack, took his camera, and snapped a photo into the night. In the sudden flash, its blinding white cutting through the duller glow of the campfire, the outline of someone standing under the branches at the edge of the woods was suddenly clear, and in an instantaneous reaction I cried some cry into the night -- but almost simultaneously with this mid-brain reaction I recognized it was only Katie Morgan standing just outside the circle of the campfire's light.

"You yelp like you've seen a ghost," she said, irritated and waving a hand in front of her blinded eyes, stepping a bit toward the fire though remaining mostly in shadow.

"Hi Katie," I said. "What do you expect, with you lurking there like that?"

She did not respond, so I continued. "What brings you out into the woods tonight?"

"I always walk in the woods at night. It's peaceful when you're not -- strobed. But tonight it is dark. So dark. Darker than you know -- yet."

That was strange – but was just Katie living up to her reputation. I kept it cheerful: "So come down by the fire with me and wait for the others. We'll tell stories."

"I'll tell you a story, if you like," she said. "A family story. A dark story. A ghost story."

"That's perfect for a campfire on a dark night. Sit down – I'll be your willing audience of one."

"I think I'd prefer to tell it from out here, on the edge of the darkness. It is more appropriate – and will have more effect."

"So, tell it then," I said. And so, she told me:

"You probably haven't heard about it before, but this little hollow on the hillside where we are talking has a history that goes way back before Ketsanis; when my family bought this land from the logging company a hundred years ago this was called the 'dry spring of the Mohawks.'

"Now, none of the Mohawk people actually lived around this

hillside, but there was a spring here on one of their paths into the high mountains, and a little river ran from it down to the lake. It was protected by a spirit sacred to them, a spirit older than all telling, older than all that is human, a spirit generous but proud, faithful but vengeful, protective if honored or death-dealing if not. And when this land was taken from her people, those who would call upon her and honor her as they took water from her spring, by others who honored only themselves, then the spirit withdrew her protection, and the spring went dry. The men who had taken the land then dug a well to force the spirit of the land to give up her water, but she was not to be thus violated, and the well itself ran dry - and we are told the men who dug it both died not long after, their hearts stopped in the night. After that no one came back again to deepen the well – a stone was placed over it, and the well-house that had been built around it fell into disuse, and time passed, and many things once known about this place were forgotten. All this was certainly forgotten by the time my family had the remains of that well-house cleared aside to build the bunk just below you there.

"You know bunk thirteen is haunted. You have heard whatever it is that is in there call to you in a borrowed voice. Before bunk thirteen, the old well-house was haunted as well. But why? What is special about this place, that ghosts are bred here?

"Ghosts, I have come to believe – and I have had time to think this through - are the absences left in the world when life is taken away. We somehow find ourselves alive, we make our noise, we die – but the eternal succession of nights and days continues; the sunlight through our windows comes and goes as before through now-empty silent rooms; undisturbed, soft movements of the air obscure with dust the once-familiar places where all that had been ours would seem to have forgotten us. Everything is as it should be, only *we are not there* -- and it is then that strangers, the passers-by outside 'our' windows, begin to speak of ghosts within.

"Yes, that is one sort of haunting – but not the only one, and not of the most disturbing kind. What about anguish? When an absence echoes with pain, will it not be more terrible? And why must it be that only *human* absence and *human* anguish should tear the fabric of the world, with 'ghosts' our name for the torn parts? Might it not be that if a fox died in some place, slowly, miserably, starving at the bottom of a well from which there was no escape, there should yet be an echo of its hunger in the restless, causeless rattling of branches on windless nights above that long-forgotten spot? Might even the pain of a spider, fed to a bird when the woods were young, be enough to start a tear in things which, drawing in later and greater accretions of pain, in time may grow large enough to become a thing of fear and earn itself a name? Perhaps that is why there is a strangeness in all deep woods, and a fear beyond that of the hunted in their dark places, echoing as they do with so many violent years, retaining perhaps in their unpeopled vastness the gestations of an inhuman anguish beyond our knowledge or even our imagination.

"In the summer of 1907, a young man who now is – absent – sat near where you are sitting, on a stone beside the well-house, listening to the rattling of branches on a windless day, listening to Blue Jay chicks in their nest in the trees above him demand victim-insects from their fierce mother, listening with an acuity he had never possessed, even though a musician, when he still possessed his sight. Two years before, he had been the prodigy child of comfortably middle-class parents, both teachers of music at Manhattan's new Institute of Musical Art. Now, he had become the charity project of society hostesses. He had lost his sight at age sixteen in the fire which had killed his parents. He was brilliant, angry, proud, scared, and suddenly alone.

"His name was Julien Sorel. Like the fictional character after whom he was named, he was short but handsome. This helped in finding him sponsors, whom he depended upon and despised in equal measure, for he could not bear dependency. A friend of his parents who taught shorthand at the Cooper Union's *Female School of Design* found Julien a tutor in the use of a Braille slate and stylus, and a charity headed up by Eva Sigursson paid for his keep at a boarding-house with a piano. Eva's idea was that Julien, who was poor now, could earn his living tuning pianos and teaching music to the blind. But there were so few scores transcribed into Braille to teach from! – and so it was that as her good work for the summer Eva decided to set up a studio in her stables at Ketsanis, where she would team Julien up with a sighted assistant (a young man on her house staff who could read music), and together they could transcribe the songs of Schubert into Braille music notation.

"So Julien came to Ketsanis and played out the part which had been scripted for him, notating his music, taking his meals with the servants, and learning his way about the compound – the stables by the lake, the Great Oak Camphouse, the walk up the logging road toward the old well-house and the deep forests beyond. When he could, he liked to brood alone in the hayloft of the stables, hauling himself up the hayloft rope hand over hand with hardly any use of his feet at all, in a show of strength which was remarked on by the stable hands and noted with interest by Eva's daughters.

"When invited to dine with his benefactor – generally on Sundays for lunch - Julien was the model of deference, perfectly modest in his conversation with his sponsor's two proud daughters, whom he resented for their wealth and unearned good fortune; they in turn had come to disregard *him* for his unthreatening mildness. Fortunately in his blindness he was not tormented by their beauty, but he was aware of it. Katrin in particular had a manner which seemed to assume her own beauty as granting her a privilege beyond question, as if to state: 'I know I am so striking that to look at me is to love me, if you are a man, or to dread my rivalry if you are a woman, so do not bore me by dwelling on such things.'

"Now, you must not assume that our Katrin was just some pretty green-eyed doll. Her beauty and her wealth gave her the freedom to be whoever she wanted to be without much social cost, and as she finished her freshman year of college she was discovering that she wanted to be something a bit more dangerous than a conventional society hostess. She played piano, as all society girls should, but her taste ran to the tonal ambivalence of late Liszt and the insinuations of Scriabin more than would be permitted if she were not socially beyond criticism. Society girls played Mendelssohn's respectable *Songs without Words*, not Scriabin's passionate and erotic *Etude in C-Sharp Minor*. She admired poetry and art, as all society girls should, but it was the perfumed poison of Swinburne's Sapphic poems and the decadence of Aubrey Beardsley that fascinated her. All her transgressions were permitted only because of the success of her late father's investments, and for the sake of her own green eyes.

"It was this attraction to dangerous passions that first made Julien a problem for Katrin. After one of their so-polite Sunday lunches, Eva invited Julien to join the family in the Great Hall of their compound for some music.

"'You have been with us for a month now,' she said. 'Come give us some of that Schubert you have been transcribing. I'll have someone fetch the music. I suppose you cannot play well since your accident, but Katie or Brynnie can play and you can sing.'

"'I can still play what I know by heart,' said Julien in a suddenly forceful voice that betrayed his inner pride, 'and surely your daughters do not need to have *Braille* music fetched.' Bryndis and Katrin looked at one another in amusement, startled that their mother's project had a little bite to him after all. Julien turned to the girls and asked 'do you know the ErlKonig?'

"'I do,' said Katrin, suddenly eager to hear what their blind border would make of one of Schubert's most difficult accompaniments.

"And what she heard did not disappoint. The rapid triplets, the repeated octaves, the controlled but surging passion of the playing all brought to life the galloping horse, the ride through night and wind – as Katrin sang she felt the energy of the accompaniment surge through her, thrill her, terrify her. She forgot her money, forgot her beauty, forgot even the blind boy with strong arms at the piano – there was nothing in the world but the music. It was only after the piano had paused and in silence she sang her final 'in her arms, the child was dead' that she returned to the world from a place she had never been before.

"Katrin looked at her mother and sister. Both were beaming, but neither seemed to have been transported to whatever transcendent plane Katrin had just returned from. 'Well done Julien! Brava, my Katie!' said Eva, entertained but not transformed. 'Now Brynnie, can you give us something? And Julien, perhaps you can let us hear *your* voice?'

"'Do you know Shubert's *Serenade*?' asked Bryndis. Julien simply stood, indicated the piano bench with a half-bow, and walked to the other end of the piano. As the song began, Julien's voice rose above the piano's gentle accompaniment in a resonant baritone utterly unlike his unremarkable speaking voice. Shubert's familiar melody had never seemed so tender; it was like hearing the voice of a mysterious suitor singing for her alone from a secluded garden at midnight:

Whispering branches softly murmur in the moonlight clear,
  In the moonlight clear;
None may watch thee, none can harm thee, wherefore dost thou fear?
  Wherefore dost thou fear?

"Listening, Katrin found herself transported once again to some pure unconventioned world where all was music – there was nothing that mattered but the song. When it was over she was surprised to find that she had cried, and for a moment felt glad that Julien was unable to see this. That cold thought passed quickly – but what did not pass was a strong conviction that she had suddenly seen who Julien *really* was – and he was *nothing* like the polite boy from the lunch table. There was something proud, passionate, and dangerous in him – and Katrin for the first time in her life found herself on the edge of love.

"But perhaps I have digressed. It was a ghost story, not a love story that I promised to tell. And for that I must go back to where I introduced my Julien to you, two months into his summer at Ketsanis, sitting near where you are sitting right now, my solitary listener, on a stone beside the well-house, listening to the inexplicable rattling of branches on a windless day.

"Since losing his sight, Julien had become expert in learning about his environment from attentive and critical listening to the sounds around him, in all their layering and subtlety. One reason he enjoyed walking up the old logging road to the little hollow above the well-house was the soundscape it offered: in the valley below him the lake, the Great Camp-House of Ketsanis, the stables, and the fields beyond all told their stories of everyday activities, which rose up the hillside and joined in counterpoint with the stories being told from the woods, as they stretched without limit up the long gentle hillside toward the high peaks beyond.

"On the day I am telling you of, a horse was being lunged in the fields below, and someone – certainly Katrin, judging from the near-professional technique – was working out some Scriabin on the piano. The Blue Jay chicks were importunate in the branches, a woodpecker was at work much deeper in the forest – and all of these together told a sensible story of the world, in which Julien could comfortably situate himself. But from just below him, beside the well-house, came a quiet, dry sound of bare branches rattling against bare branches, a sound of windy winter on this windless summer day. Julien was entirely focused on this sound, as it was the one thing he could not understand, a foreign and unexplained intrusion in his soundscape which for all its subtlety disturbed him. Was it the doings of squirrels, leaping from branch to branch on a dead tree? Or of branches snapping back on one another as birds perched and then flew away? He tried theory after theory, but none fit. And as he was doing this, he became aware of a new sound, a slow grating as of a heavy stone sliding over stones, from the well-house itself.

"Interested, Julien picked up his cane and walked down to the well-house. This was a small wooden building, older than anything else in Ketsanis and not in good repair, as the well had long been dry and the well-house disused. A single door which no longer quite closed, with one dirty but intact casement window to the left side when entering - led into a single room. To the right on entering was the stone circle of the well, perhaps two feet high, capped by a large stone which would require two men to move. Some iron loops which must have been part of the old well apparatus were attached at four points around the well's base. To the left were a few wooden crates, an old bucket, and on the wall the loops of a thick and solid rope, with iron hooks at its ends, again presumably part of the old well apparatus.

"Julien pushed open the door and stepped in. He still heard the rattling of branches outside the well-house, but the grating sound had stopped. Julien had not been in the well-house before, and slowly with hand and cane he explored it. He had expected to find it a nest of spiders, but was puzzled to find the place web-free and almost without the feel of dust. Why this should be in a place he understood to have been out of use for a half century was another element of this place which seemed to be without explanation. The room was also *entirely* soundless – there was no sound of even the subtlest sort save that which came from outside – and that, save the rattling of branches overhead, seemed strangely muffled. Then, as he stood remarking on this to himself, there it was again: that slow grating sound. It was clearly from the well, as though the well-cap was being pushed slowly over the stones of the well on which it lay. That would mean: he could not be alone in here. Someone – someone who could maintain a *perfect* silence – was in here with him. A sudden chill ran through his body, as if the temperature about him had dropped twenty degrees. There could be no good reason for a person to hold themselves in silence, undisclosed, in this way. He had to get out of there. And then he heard it as faint as could be in the midst of silence – one word: 'Julie?'

"He burst toward the door, tripped over his own cane and landed hard on the ground just outside the well-house. But even as he was falling, his mind put things in order and he recognized the voice. It was his mother's.

"He rolled from his fall as quickly as he could, as if in some sort of combat, and faced the door crouching, feeling with his foot for his cane, which once found he brandished toward the well-house as if it were a weapon. He stood that way for perhaps a minute, listening, waiting, prepared to attack or to flee, as his mind raced. His mother's voice! That was impossible. But he had no doubt of it – his mother had called him, by a name only she had used and which he had not heard in the two years since the fire.

"Nothing happened. He waited, but there was no further sound from the well-house. He noted that the rattling of branches had ceased as well. Everything was poised in expectation. He wanted to run. As soon as he dared move, he would keep his face to the well-house and back down the hill as quickly as he could. But – his mother's voice! He *had* heard it. Did that mean that – she was not dead? That - death was not the end of everything? That – he was not alone, not abandoned in a world which was just a cruel and pointless carnival of pain and shattered dreams whose only exit was to obliteration and utter annihilation?

"Then – there it was again – the grating sound from inside the well-house. Whatever it was, it was starting again. Now was the time to run. But – his mother's voice! Would he really run from the possibility that in some sense she still continued with him? Was he such a coward as that? If he could ask for any blessing from the world, would it not be this, to know with certainty that his parents had survived death, that he would survive death, that *we all* would survive death; that this world is a deeper and more wonderful place than he could have hoped or imagined? Would this not be better even than the return of his sight? And he wanted to run *from this*? Only a coward would not embrace it! Within the well-house he again heard the grating sound. With terror, utter terror, in his heart, he stepped through the door and into the well-house. With a bang the door shut behind him, and the cold gripped him. But, in the darkness of his blindness, he just stood there, listening, and asked 'mother?' of the empty air.

"Nothing happened. Again all was silence. He waited, watchful. Then, again, he heard the grating sound, louder now, and then louder still, almost violent, before all was silence again. He waited, but nothing further ensued. The cold had passed, and he heard the sounds of the Jay chicks from outside. He stretched his hand toward the door, and found that it had soundlessly opened. He pushed it, and found that as at first it would not entirely close. The terror was draining out of him. He went over to the wellhead to sit down -- and suddenly was filled with a sickening nausea as he felt *nothing* beneath him where the well cap stone should be. Trying to stand again, but falling, he pushed off with his hand against the well itself and flung himself forward, hitting his back on the well but landing on the ground. When he rose, he very carefully felt his way around the wellhead. The capping stone had slid almost half way off its base, and the well itself was in large part exposed. But nothing further happened.

"After half an hour, Julien left, and walked back down the old logging road, his mind a rush of confusions, thinking thoughts he had never dared to think before. He knew he would go back every day until his mother spoke to him again. He knew that somehow this was why he had been brought to Ketsanis. He knew he had been offered a gift, if he dared to take it.

"And so, in the last month of Julien's summer, he would no longer be found hauling himself up the ropes to the barn-loft, or spending more time than the minimum needed on his Braille music transcriptions. When he could, he would go up to the well-house, and call 'mother?' into the silence, and wait. His waiting was not unrewarded – the well-cap, which had returned itself to its usual position over the wellhead, would often be pushed about by unseen hands; increasingly often, Julien would hear a soft pop in some corner of the wellhouse, and when investigating this Julien sometimes found objects – pebbles, a coin, a large serving spoon – inexplicably dropped in the location from which the popping sound had come. Julien collected everything he found this way in the bucket beneath the old well-rope. The sheer strangeness of all this kept Julien as scared as he was excited, though over time his terror grew less as these things became almost familiar.

"What did *not* become familiar were the voices. Usually they were too soft to hear distinctly, and it was not clear whether they were always entirely human. Sometimes they were fragments, as on one day when he heard 'must end this' in what may have been his father's voice, overlapping 'he is ours' in a voice he did not know. The most disturbing of these voices spoke to him one night when he dared to go to the wellhouse late on a night when he could not sleep. Immediately upon entry everything had grown cold, and the grating of the wellcap grew violent, exposing the well almost in full. As Julien stood beside the open well, feeling its extent with his cane and dropping in some of his 'popped' pebbles to get a sense for its depth (which did not appear too great), a voice situated over the well, or perhaps within it, said quite clearly 'I will shelter you forever.' But it was not his mother's voice, nor his father's, and it scared him out of further night-visits despite all his resolutions to be brave.

"Now, all of this had begun shortly after Eva's first invitation for Julien to perform with her daughters on Sunday afternoons, which in the last month of the summer became a regular weekly event. Perhaps the one thing not overshadowed in Julien's heart by his search for eternity in the wellhouse was his passion for performance, and so it was that every week brought a fresh reminder to Katrin and Bryndis, but most especially Katrin, that he was something different in kind from the other young men they knew. Every Sunday, Katrin would fall in love again, and then she would have a week to recover by reminding herself of Julien's poverty and blindness. But Julien's very indifference to her was disturbing, as it was unique in her experience of young men. As Julien grew more and more occupied with some obsession unknown to her it was clear to Katrin that his passions were directed elsewhere – which was an unprecedented challenge and provocation which kept Julien present in her mind far more than she would wish him to be. Katrin had even gone up to the wellhouse one day to try to learn what it was that attracted Julien to that place, but found nothing of any interest at all, save the puzzlement of one of her mother's serving spoons stashed away in the old well bucket. This was a greater disappointment than she fully admitted to herself. She had wanted to find a tell-tale sign, some keepsake of her to show that he was as enamored of her as every other young man she'd met. Instead, she had found – a spoon.

"And so it was that as the summer drew to its close everything was unresolved. Julien had received no convincing revelation from his parents; Katrin had given no indication to Julien that she even recognized his existence when they were not performing together. The day had come when Katrin would leave to go back to school, and soon after that, Julien would leave to begin making his way as a piano-tuner and teacher of music to the blind in New York City. He would never learn if his mother's spirit had really called his name. Katrin would never learn if the passion she and Julien had shared as music could be realized on Earth as Love.

"The day was Tuesday, the third of September, 1907. Katrin was returning to Radcliffe for her sophomore year; Bryndis would be leaving for Barnard the following day. Katrin had said goodbye to her mother, and a coachman had driven her and her luggage in a light little trap down to the station at Lake Ohneka, where she awaited her train to Saratoga, with connections on to New York and finally to Boston. She had checked her luggage on through to Boston, and was pretending to read a fashion magazine while in fact obsessing about leaving Julien without even a good-bye. The longer she waited, the more she obsessed, until after some while it was announced that her train was cancelled due to rail troubles up the line, and all passengers would have to wait for an afternoon train, expected in five hours' time.

"Katrin decided that she now had time for an hour's walk back to Ketsanis to resolve things with Julien. He would probably be at his precious wellhouse. She would ask him to visit her in Cambridge to perform something together. She would find out if he felt anything for her at all. Maybe they would confess love to each other, or maybe she would just be able to say good-bye and that would be that, forever.

"Julien, meanwhile, had gone up to the wellhouse also looking to bring things to a conclusion. If he had been brought to Ketsanis to find this place that somehow connected the world of the living to – well, to something he could not understand but had once spoken to him in his mother's voice, then it made no sense for things to end as they were: ambiguous and frustrated, without conviction, meaning, or resolution. At dawn he went up the hill along the old mining road, the old Mohawk trail to Tahawus the cloud-splitter and bringer of visions, and with no fear he entered the wellhouse, fell to his knees, and begged: 'If in this place you who are dead may live, then show yourselves to me; if all I understand to have been taken from me has only been borrowed for a while – O, father! O, mother! O, sight! -- then instruct me, convince me in a way I cannot doubt so in peace I shall be content to wait; if in this place those who are torn apart can again be brought together, then let me *hear*, let me *feel*, let me -- *see* that I am not alone!'

"But the only answer Julien received was silence. The sun shone through the window of the wellhouse; a light breeze through the open door stirred what little dust there was on the rope and crates beside him, but no sign was given from the shadows, and no voice whispered secrets beyond the knowledge of mankind from the empty air.

"Julien stood his ground. He begged in silence. The minutes and hours passed, but he maintained his intensity. At last he heard the rattling sound of branches in the trees above the wellhouse, the familiar grating of the capstone over the wellhead stones, the disturbing whispers in the cooling air. But this, which had once been terrifying, now only enraged him. 'What damned pointless show is this?' he cried aloud. 'Is this the best you can do? You are beneath contempt! Trivial! Weak! I am through with you!' He stood to go. All this was over. He would pack his things and return to New York, to tune the pianos of society girls who could barely even play and who would never give themselves entirely to the passions of unfettered music; he would be alone and he would be poor and then he would die, and death would be a blessing, and he would welcome it.

"But even as he rose to stand there was a sudden fierce cold about him, and the door slammed with a bang which shook the walls, and the grating of the wellcap surged in a roar as the great stone was flung near off the wellhead, and there was a great clatter as the rope hung on the wall was suddenly flung all about, and in the darkness of his blindness Julien felt cold hands on his arms and face and chest and thighs and groin, caressing him loathsomely. He was stark with fear, for a moment, but then a rage greater than his fear filled him and he called out once more: 'Again you fail me! What pointless corruption is this? This is not what I have asked of you! Give me what I have asked – what I have *earned*!' and in that moment all the loathsome touching ceased and a tingling as of great electrical energy filled the room and his mother's voice cried out 'O my brave boy! Now I am permitted to give you what you have deserved: here is your independence and your freedom, and my warrant that you shall never again be alone, forever.'

"Then with shocking suddenness all was gone – the cold, the electric charge, the voice, the rattling of branches and stones and all sounds utterly save a single sharp 'pop' in the air just before him and, almost immediately, a small clatter on the ground below. Julien reached down and grasped a ring, almost hot to the touch but quickly cooling: a ring, Julien could feel, with a quite large stone set in it.

"'Julien?'

"Another voice had broken the silence. Julien was briefly dizzied – this voice confused him; it seemed unconnected to everything else.

"'Julien!'

"He recognized the voice as Katrin's. She had appeared from nowhere and suddenly stepped into the wellhouse. She was looking about her at the chaos – the rope on the floor, the well-cap stone hurled to the side of the open wellhead, Julien standing in the midst of all this, holding –

"'My mother's ring?'

"Katrin was shocked. In Julien's hand was her mother's engagement ring, several carats of the finest diamond a society engagement could call for. Katrin had hunted down Julien to confess her love, only to find – a thief? Is this what all his doings in the wellhouse were about? Had he stashed whatever he had secretly made off with all summer long up here, and now that the summer was over he was retrieving the goods? She dashed forward suddenly and snatched the ring out from Julien's hand.

"Julien hardly knew what was happening. His mother had spoken to him, had given him a ring summoned from empty air to be his fortune and his return to independence – then suddenly Katrin was there and ... and it was at that point that he felt the ring snatched out of his fingers. 'No!' he cried and leaped forward to grab it back, felt the crash of his left shoulder into something warm, which gave way before him – and then there was a piercing shriek, a brief clattering by the wellhead, something of a deep thump and quiver of the floorboard beneath his feet, and silence. He did not know what had happened. He could not understand.

"And then, in a moment, he understood the story of this soundscape. He had crashed into Katrin. She had fallen backward down the well. He was – he was a murderer.

"He released a howl of shock and pain which almost tore his lungs as he fell to his knees and beat his hands against his forehead. Then, suddenly, he stopped, and with all the intensity of his passionate spirit he listened into the silence and begged whatever Gods there are or have ever been for any sound from the well, any indication that Katrin might yet be alive. But the silence was absolute and unbroken. Julien waited. Julien prayed. But there was perfect silence from the well. And then, above in the trees, came the rattling of branches. It was like an insult. Julien burst into tears and collapsed upon the floor.

"I do not know how much time then passed. Perhaps it was minutes, perhaps it was an hour. For Julien it was simply a cessation, and then something like a re-formation of himself, with no clear notion of the interval in between. When he returned to himself what he felt was something close to – anger. He had overcome his fears and obtained convincing proof that his mother, in some form, still was watching over him. She had brought him a gift, a ring of great worth, to free him from the dependency he so despised, to rescue him from a life of meaningless and trivial labors, to give him the leisure to return to his love affair with music. And then this girl had appeared and it was all over. She was dead now, and he was a murderer. His life was over. He felt around him on the ground with his hands. The ring was not there. It had gone down with her, into the well.

"And then, the most dreadful of thoughts suggested itself to him: the well was not deep; good strong rope was strewn about him on the floor; the climb down into the well and up again would be no harder than the climb up the hayloft rope at the stables. Why shouldn't he go down into the well and recover the ring? Just because he was – afraid? Was he that weak? His mother had returned from what unknowable distance in the vastnesses of death to bring him a final gift, his independence and his future, and through his own cowardice would he throw this gift away? He would not. He would retrieve the ring. He would take it, and vanish, and never be Julien Sorel again, and would make a new life far away, and would not let himself be defeated by this. He reached out and found the metal hook at one end of the rope strewn about him. He fastened it to a metal ring at the base of the wellhead and lowered the rope into the well until it hit – whatever lay there at the bottom. He tugged hard at it, and it was solid. He prepared to climb down.

"Now, my solitary listener, I must ask you: can you imagine this that you are hearing? Have you ever been in the dark with the dead? Perhaps in a house with a corpse in it, after night has fallen, and with no one else around? Rational as you may be, were you — or would you be -- unafraid? I did not think so. The dead are uncanny, and despite ourselves we fear them. But imagine then that the body is not just any body, but the body of someone you yourself have killed? That the house is not just any house, but one where you know the dead have been – wakeful? That the room you are in is not just any room, but the small circumference of a well, so you and this body will be up close as tight as lovers? If you can imagine this, then you are prepared for me to take you down the well with Julien ... to Katrin.

"As Julien hung his feet over the inside edge of the well, and took the rope in his hands, he was in such terror that his hands were numb and he was unsure whether he could sufficiently hold his weight. Still, he would not turn back, and after the first moment of descent his terror eased. He was blind, so he did not experience his climb as a descent into darkness, but he felt the closeness of the air and the coolness of the stones and earth circled about him, and a claustrophobia he never knew he possessed began to course through him. Still down he went. After some while, the descent began to become almost routine. And then, he felt something flap against his ankle, and he startled, almost losing his grip on the rope. He was almost at the bottom of the well, and one of Katrin's feet, projecting into the air, had brushed against him. She had fallen head first, and lay upside down at the bottom, neck to the ground, head snapped to the side. She had been unable to raise her arms before she had gone down the well; they, like her feet, projected upwards toward Julien in his final descent. At the end, he had to squeeze beside Katrin's body till his feet stood on stony ground beside her head. Her body, upside down, occupied half the width of the well. They were indeed as close as lovers.

"He stood at the bottom. Now to get what he came for he had to find the ring. Was it – still in her hand? This would be terrible. Her hands were at the level of his stomach. He took her cooling hands in his – feeling for the ring. It was not there. Had it fallen to the ground below? Did she have time to pocket it before he had knocked her backward down the well?

"As he stood wondering what to do next he thought he heard some of that half-inhuman whispering which he had often heard in the wellhouse. He had never grown comfortable with it above; it was still more disturbing at the bottom of the well, and he froze. It was hard to breathe, and his knees were weak. But to business – there was not enough room to bend down and feel for the ring at the bottom of the well – Katrin's upper body was filling too much of that space. He tried to feel with his foot – would he need to take off his shoe for more sensitivity? Much of the well's floor was on the far side of Katrin's head; could he just – kick her head out of the way? Julien was sickened with the thought of it, and, more practically, it would be ineffective. Even pressing hard against Katrin's body he could not explore all of the floor space, and his foot even without its shoe might not be sensitive enough to tell a stone from a ring. He would have to lift Katrin up, to get down underneath her.

"He was breathing hard. He was claustrophobic and terrified and the air at the bottom of the well was not good. He tried lifting Katrin by her clothing because he dreaded the cold touch of her flesh, but as he lifted her, her body began to pull loose from her clothing and her arms and legs flapped about him, jamming into the rough encircling sides of the well so he could not lift her. He grabbed her directly beneath her shoulders, which rested on the well-bottom, and as he leaned back he shoved her upwards as hard as he could. She wound up bent double, curled like a fetus, facing him with her thighs cradled in the crook of his elbows against his chest, his arms supporting her back, her chest toward him at the level of his face, and her legs up in the air above his shoulders. From that position, he thought he could lift her briefly with one great push more, duck underneath her, and bend down with her weight on his back to explore the bottom of the well for the ring on his hands and knees.

"But suddenly, he heard a voice, and everything changed. It was a voice he had heard before, weeks ago when hoping to contact his mother's spirit in the wellhouse. It was a stranger's voice, and it said: 'he is ours.'

"At once his terror spiked again. Pressed tight against this woman he had murdered, at the bottom of a well, claustrophobia gripped him entirely and he began to gasp for air. His hands and arms were shaking. He felt faint. And suddenly with perfect clarity he realized: the air was bad down at the bottom of the well. He could hardly continue to hold Katrin's body in his arms. He could never have the strength to climb back out of the well again. He would die down here.

"At that his whole body tensed in shock and fear. His heart beat irregularly, his head swam. He could no longer hold Katrin's body in the position he had her, and as she slid slowly down against the stones of the well her legs seemed to grip either side of his chest, her arms fell over his shoulders, and her broken face descended to the level of his.

"And it was then that our Julien, our *blind* Julien, began to sense something like a glow about him in the wellshaft. Could he – see? Swiftly it became unambiguous, there *was* light about him, and in that light there was Katie, ravishing Katie *whom he had never before seen*, Katie of the fair hair and perfect Burne-Jones face and provoking green eyes, Katie in all her almost supernatural beauty before him. But as she looked at him with eyes that seemed to be still living there came a change, and her head dropped to the side of her neck, turning up her lips as if to kiss, but grotesquely, all out of alignment, as the blood which had rushed to her face as she lay upside down in the well with her neck broken blackened her complexion and puffed out her now-filmy eyes, and soon what he saw was the corpse he had created in all its horror and ruin, and its arms closed tight about him and from its blacked lips came the last words Julien would ever hear: 'I could have loved you, you who were so alone – but see, *see* what you have done to me …'

"Julien shut his eyes – which made no difference. He was blind. What he was experiencing was something that had nothing to do with sight. He clawed at his face with his hands, gouged at his eyes until they were torn and his face ran with blood, but nothing could interrupt his vision. From the bottom of the depths into which he had been led he shrieked, and shrieked again, and then suddenly lurched forward and was silent.

"Julien's heart had stopped. His corpse lay at the bottom of the well shaft, entwined with the body of the woman who had loved him, and whom he had killed. Above him, in the wellhouse, all was quiet. The rope, as if loosed by an invisible hand, came free from its iron ring and slipped almost gracefully into the dark of the well. A grating sound of heavy stone over stones briefly replaced the muffled shrieks that had been echoing from the well, as the great capping stone slid back to its rightful place. Time passed. The sunlight through the wellhouse window shone gently through the now-empty silent room; undisturbed, soft movements of the air obscured with lightest dust all evidence of struggle. Everything was again as it should be, only *Katrin and Julien were not there*."

AT THE CAMPFIRE – ALONE

The story was over. The fire had burned very low; it had become little more than a glow of embers. The storyteller stood just outside the shrunken circle of firelight, silent, as she was before I had snapped her picture. A tension, a strange expectancy, was in the air between us. I did not know what to say, but I tried to defuse the tension: "Well done, Katie!" I said, "but it's a good thing I know that story can't be true, or I'd *never* go near bunk thirteen again."

"And how do you know it is not true?"

"With all the witnesses dead at the bottom of a well, who is left who could tell it?"

"Perhaps I have heard it at the campfires of the dead," said the storyteller. But what came next no longer seemed merely Katie being Katie: "What sort of tales do you suppose are told by the dead to the dead around the embers of your campfires after you have retreated to your beds? The most terrible of stories are known only to we who are dead, for none who are living have experienced the worst of things."

And as she said this I found myself aware that we two were not alone around the campfire. Other shapes seemed to be revealing themselves as densities of complete darkness against the forest night. Then the fire's faint glow began to catch them, and implications of face and form began to emerge. There were so many of them – so many Brynns and Katies, though there were also others who bore no resemblance to them. Still others – dim, feral shapes of shadow – did not seem to be human at all. In fact, there was a certain inhumanity about all of them, as though being no longer among the living had freed them from keeping up appearances, and something ancient, cold, implacable that was in them all along, in *all of us*, had begun to emerge, to show itself through their veneer of humanity. But human or not, as they became distinct and unambiguous I noted that they were all turned toward me – or perhaps toward a place just over my left shoulder ...

At once I spun about, and there not two feet before me stood Julien Sorel - or what was left of what had once been he. He stood there, head bowed with hands on his forehead, resembling myself so much that I startled, *but with no eyes at all*, having merely a sunken smoothness of skin where his eyes had been. He was an overwhelming vortex of anguished despair – the terror I felt was nothing so much as a horror that our world could permit such anguish. I felt something draw close behind me, but frozen in the blast of the insanity of misery that was Julien I found I could hardly move. Still somehow I turned - and only then did I realize there was a greater shadow connecting all around the campfire, like a web in which they were all enmeshed. Something of that web of darkness was what I had felt approaching behind me -- a darkness without human form that slowly developed a hand or *paw or feeler* of dark silver night that reached toward me, and above it a subtle silvering of the darkness which suggested at once the stalked eyes of a spider and the alert face of a fox.

Whatever it was, it did not speak, it *could* not speak, and yet it was as if it had a direct connection to my mind, and as it drew about me I *felt* what it seemed to want me to know: "Come bring me your terror, over-proud intruder; I will feast on your mind, and in the emptiness where I have fed will be madness, and your madness will be the measure of my appetite. Do you think that we who are dead have lost all power? Do you believe that fear is all we who are beyond anything you can understand can visit upon you? Do you expect that if I reach out my hand to strike, it will pass though you and be harmless? No, that is not the way of things, nothing that walks this world by day or night can be so impotent. With my dead hand I can indeed reach through you – reach into your chest and grasp your beating heart while you stand frozen in a fear whose paralysis is also among my powers over you – and if I grasp your heart the cold of death will wrap about it and chill it, and you will feel it flutter as it fails, and you will stagger as it stops – and what survives of you will be taken into me. I have taken so many to myself since you people have come to my land and cut in me my wound. Tonight, why should I not take you?"

But as this loathsome – thing – drew about me, a night-rending shriek rose from the valley below, and a moment later it was followed by the report of a gunshot through glass, more cries in the night, the slamming of cabin doors, and feet on the old camp road. Before me, all the watchful shadows that had gathered about the campfire of the dead turned toward the great camphouse, and the deeper darkness surrounding me filled with a dreadful exultation and was gone, taking with it all else caught in its web. Far away in the soundscape of the night, I heard the shriek of Bryndis Morgan calling the name of her daughter, who had just been interrupted in an attempt on her own life, and who had just performed an update to that same suicide note re-used across generations, asking that there be an end to Katies, to which she had signed a third name, below her Grandmother's and Katie Eastman's.

I fell to my knees, all alone beside the now-extinguished campfire, and my eyes fixed almost sightlessly on the Polaroid of the storyteller I had taken for Katie Morgan – who clearly could *not* have been telling me any stories around the campfire that evening. It was only when I showed the photo to Astrid later by better light that I saw the eyes of Katrin Sigursson, pure Icelandic green just as in her portrait, and as cold as a glacier's ice, still angry for the wreckage of her once-happy life, looking back at me from the photograph.

2 THE CLEANSING OF KETSANIS

THE PROPHET OF THE WELL

Every camp has its ghost stories – as, I suppose, does every castle, inn, or other settled place where life and death have played through generations and we the living find ourselves performing in theatres which long before have staged the stories of the dead. How deeply strange is this, our world, when we look into its dark places! How much stranger still would we find it could we travel with the winds through trackless forests, with the currents through deepest seas -- freed from the safe boundaries of our little selves -- and learn the inhuman secrets of all that in fear or malice wait out the squall that is mankind? For we who would get on with the business of living, for at least a little while longer, with homes to maintain and gardens to tend and illusions of security to preserve, perhaps it is best there are things we can never know and stories we will never be told.

But that is no excuse to leave what tales we *do* know of greater things unfinished, if what remains to tell can shine light into darkness – or even give us cause to hope that understanding, redemption, and joy may yet remain when all boundaries are removed.

On that night when Katie Morgan almost took her own life, and mine was almost lost to a web of shadows I will never fully understand, I found myself a prophet, to whom the secrets of the well beneath Bunk Thirteen had been revealed, through whom all must be retold with a tongue of fire. But the time for prophesy had not yet come. A mother was in despair that her only daughter might

29

yet succeed in self-destruction, and a father had seen the ruin of all his plans -- for was the whole motive force of Camp Ketsanis not just his quest to find a way to help a daughter he feared would take the path of her grandmother and cousin, suicides both, into death? The tale I had to tell was a family story, but the family that needed to hear it was not yet ready.

On that night, fleeing from the campfire of the dead, as half the counselors at camp were calming their excited charges and half were on the old camp road relaying gossip as to what was going down in the Great Camphouse, I found Astrid and told her my story. I showed her my Polaroid of Katrin Sigursson on the edge of the forest, and then we went together back up to the fire-ring above bunk thirteen. There was so much action on the road, so much adolescent excitement in the air, that we felt no fear where not long before my life had been in jeopardy. Chris's backpack and camera were still beside the fire-ring, but there was no fire – nor any warmth indicating there had ever been a fire there that night (and of course Chris later insisted he had not been so great an ass as to leave a fire untended). Astrid and I debated whether even the fire I had sat myself beside had been something unnatural; it had felt real enough to me, but that, it would seem, means nothing in this world when you are on the edge of the darkness. I will never know what of that night was 'real'; I do know Astrid and I were excited, alone and nineteen – and were this another kind of tale I would have further stories to tell you of that night than I will tell here. Suffice it to say that the next day Astrid and I, like Chris and Karen, were a camp couple.

Only very late that night did Astrid and I find Chris and Karen. They had indeed been off in the woods, and knew nothing of any shrieks from the Great Camphouse until they had returned. It was Chris who advised me that Manly Morgan was not the sort who would want to hear ghost stories from me on the night of his only daughter's attempted suicide. What's more, I should not tell my story to anyone else, or rumors of it would reach the Morgans prematurely and in the wrong way. However, Chris said Manly was a man more passionate than he would admit about helping his daughter, and what I could tell him might help her – so it would not be long before the time would be right. Give it a couple of days, let Mrs. Morgan and Katie mend a little, and Chris would help me bring my story to Manly.

LUIGI

In the meanwhile, camp life continued – or perhaps I should say, it was all our jobs to make sure it continued – in as ordinary a fashion as possible. Bummer and I rousted our charges and set them to swimming and soccer; Chris and Karen kept control of their upper six campers and broke up their hourly attempts to fight with one another. In bunk one, Astrid continued her attempts to make contact with the most passive of campers, and in particular with one camper who had been assigned to her as a special charge by Manly, a regressive-autistic young Haitian boy of ten, who had forgotten the existence of all others save himself, and who was named Luigi.

Luigi was a small boy, black as obsidian, who after the death of his mother when he was six had over three month's time given up speaking to schoolmates, then friends, then even his father and brothers. Now he watched television, slapped his arms when he was happy or upset, repeated what he heard said around him, and talked word salad in English and Haitian at a Shindana *Natra* cloth-rag doll he would not be without. I could never replicate Luigi's patter for you, had Astrid not noted some down that I still retain. For hours at a time he spoke to his doll like this:

"Lionel trains, gen pa efreye, take it easy, take it easy, Green Acres sponsored by Kelloggs in the morning, don't hit yourself it is bad manners, it takes a thief, it takes Dristan capsules with maximum strength, mwen se nouvo mama ou, gen pa efreye, Hawaii Five-O sponsored by Timex, do not touch the cigar, you are a pain in the neck, Green Acres is the place to be ..."

When in the first weeks of camp Manly had asked Astrid to make a special effort to reach Luigi, she had asked what his diagnosis was.

"Atypical late-onset regressive autism," said Manly, as if reciting from a text, "but that's just diagnostic bullshit for 'nobody knows'. You know what autism means; regressive just means he was doing fine and then lost all the social skills he'd been learning and regressed back into the lost child he is today. That's known to happen – up to around age three. But Luigi was fine till he was six and his mom died. So we call it atypical, but that just means we know nothing at all about what happened."

"Can he get along with the other campers?" asked Astrid, unsure how her vigor and athleticism could possibly be brought to bear to help a child like this.

"He'll go through the motions with them. He'll dress himself, he'll take his meals – he'll read aloud all the chemicals in your cereal from the side of the box at breakfast. He'll follow your bunk to their activities and talk to his doll while they're playing. But it will be like none of you are there to him."

"But how can I help, then?" pleaded Astrid. "Shouldn't someone with a condition so – severe – be at a different kind of camp?"

Manly's eyes flashed. "We are the *only* camp for him. After us, he'll be back on medication in some institution where he will be forgotten, until some day when he's been left to piss in his own self-inflicted wounds he's carried off by septicemia and that will be the end of Luigi. I know he's still in there *somewhere*; this is something to do with the loss of his mother -- he's cut himself off from the world, but he cannot have vanished inside himself altogether. I'm looking for you to find him, Astrid, find him and bring him back."

Even fail-free Astrid Arnheim felt that this was a challenge beyond hope of accomplishment, and indeed for the first month of camp Luigi sleep-walked through the activities of camp in an isolation so impenetrable as to seem past hope of any engagement. But then there was an incident – one evening while walking back to bunk with his cabin-mates and counselors, talking word-salad to his Natra doll, he bobbled the doll and down it fell, into a rain-wash gully of about three feet's depth at the side of the path. As Luigi saw this, with a happy grace as if diving into gentle waters he lightly flung himself off the side of the path to retrieve his doll. As Astrid watched in shock, he hit the ground with face and shoulder, and tumbled to the bottom of the ditch, where he lay with an astonished look on his bloodied face. Astrid leapt down the slope behind him and felt the contour of his shoulder for broken bones. He was fine, though shocked. His cheek was torn, but not severely. He looked up at her and said "Luigi hurt." She returned his doll to him, helped him up the gully's slope, and cleaned his face.

That evening she was summoned to the Great Camphouse for a talk with Manly Morgan. She was expecting a tongue-lashing. Who knows how badly hurt Luigi could have been? She had been lucky, but a counselor who relied on luck to keep her campers safe belonged at some other camp. However - this was not what happened at all. Manly met her with the biggest of grins.

"I have heard everything!" he boomed. "'Luigi hurt' he said. Was he looking at you when he said it?"

"Right in my eyes," answered Astrid, confused. "Why do you ask?"

"Don't you know what happened today, counselor?" asked Manly in his best military manner. "Luigi spoke – *to you*. He referred to *himself* and spoke *to you*. He *told you* he was hurt. You exist, Astrid! He knows who he is, and he knows you exist!"

Astrid was suddenly filled with a sort of joy at the way Manly was reading this. "You are right! What do you want me to do?" she asked.

"I want you to run that kid up and down every mountain and push him into every ditch you find, until he speaks to you again! This is what Ketsanis is all about – when you're hurt in a ditch you can't look to some rag doll for help – you have to come out of yourself and get real."

That night it was Astrid who had the prize story at the campfire. This was truly Manly at his manliest. But in the following weeks there was no second breakthrough, and as we waited for the Morgans to be ready to hear my story of Katie and Julien, Astrid worked with Luigi in ever-lessening hope that she – or anyone – could help him find his way back from the dark journey he had taken to the strange and private cloister of his life.

REVELATIONS

It was almost two weeks after the night of the campfire of the dead that Chris pulled me aside one afternoon to tell me that he had broached the subject of my experience at bunk thirteen with Manly Morgan. Katie had returned from whatever undisclosed location she had been taken to after her suicide attempt, and though we counselors saw no more of her than we had previously, the word was that both she and her mother had returned to a semblance of happiness and a watchful sort of trust. Manly as well seemed to be once more himself, his natural force having overcome what had been reported as a despair that he could not protect his daughter from the crises that so often seemed to intercept and destroy the lives of the women in her family when they reached Katie's age. With the Morgan family at least superficially returned to normality, Chris felt the time had come for me to share my story with them. He had half-expected Manly to laugh him out of the room with his talk of ghosts, but Manly heard the outline of the tale with a surprisingly open mind. At the end, he asked Chris to tell me I was invited to come by the family quarters in the Great Camphouse that evening, and that he was eager to hear what I had to say.

I was equally eager to say it. Over the almost two weeks that my story had been pent up in me I had begun to feel it almost like an independent thing within me that was urgently seeking expression. It was accompanied by a nagging sense of something I had forgotten, like a word at the tip of the tongue that could not be found, which I attributed to an anxiety that I would forget key details of the experience.

So, that evening after the campers of bunk four were in their beds and Bummer was once more comfortably in control, I walked down the old camp road and up the opposing hill to the Great Camphouse. The lights of the Great Hall were darkened, save for one small light above the Sargent painting, and the administrative offices were closed. The only light came from the family quarters. As I passed by it, I could not help looking up at Sargent's portrait of Katrin and Bryndis. I could hardly myself believe the story I was about to tell of that girl, dead so long ago, whose painted green eyes looked down at me in the dimness. Who was I to tell such stories of her? An intruder, a busybody, a stranger of no import. I almost felt I should turn about and leave. But the story I had to tell still burned too bright within me; I walked past the painting and knocked on the door to the Morgans' quarters.

A servant opened the door and led me through a long hallway to a large room of local granite and solid Adirondack Oak where Bryndis and Matthew Morgan were awaiting me beside a small fire in a large rough stone fireplace. It was a room of rustic furniture, animal pelt rugs, Native American artifacts, mounted trophies of game, and – strangely – Japanese screens that separated the large room into several more comfortably-sized spaces. As I entered, Bryndis Astor-Morgan rose to greet me. By reputation she was very ill, though no one knew with what, but she did not seem so very ill as she walked toward me.

"So kind of you to join us this evening, Mr. Chase," she said, as if I were my dad. "Would you care for some tea? Or hot cider, perhaps? It is still summer, but here in the mountains the nights are already growing cold."

Mr. Morgan came up beside her and shook my hand. I must not call him 'Manly' I reminded myself. "I am told you would like us to believe some ghost story," he said.

I froze for a moment. This was not going to be easy. But then Mr. Morgan smiled and said "I would like to show you something."

He took me to a table beside the fireplace on which he had set nine padlocks, all locked, of various sizes. I was puzzled. "What are these?" I asked.

"They are the padlocks of bunk thirteen," he said. "Every year before camp begins I lock it up. Every year I wake up some morning to find the padlock, unopened and unharmed, lying in that big fireplace below the portrait in the Great Hall. At first, I thought it was some prank of my counselors. But I have come to realize that it is not. Even my best from the upper six each year, young men like your friend Mr. Hicey, even they are not good enough to pull off such a prank each year."

I stared at the padlocks. I was not quite sure what Mr. Morgan was getting at.

He recognized I wasn't getting it. So he looked me in the eyes and said "I am telling you, Michael, that even if you have a strange story to tell, I am prepared to hear it."

A servant came in with some cider, and as I took it I saw that the Morgans and I had been quietly joined by their daughter Katie.

Here was the young woman whom I had mistaken the ghostly Katrin Sigursson for. Looking at her closely, she was much like the girls in the double-portrait, more Bryndis of the gentle blue eyes than cat-eyed Katrin, but even apart from the eyes she was clearly not their twin. Her softer jaw made her less the *Mirror of Venus* of Burne-Jones than a blonde edition of Emma Hamilton – with her long hair loose about her shoulders, held back from her face by a headband, she was save for shade of hair and eyes the image of Romney's *Lady-Hamilton-as-Bacchante*. She wore a white empire-style sleeveless dress, with low neckline and shoulders bare, but with a gold Indian shawl draped loosely over them, like Madame Récamier as painted by Gérard, save for Katie's more modest placement of her shawl.

Katie did not waste time. "You say my great-great-aunt Katrin did not steal her mother's ring and elope one summer day?"

"She did not," I said. "She was murdered. Accidentally murdered but murdered nonetheless. She lies at the bottom of a well beneath the floorboards of bunk thirteen."

Bryndis sat back down in her chair, looking more ill now. Manly just looked toward me, awaiting more. It was Katie who continued: "And the young man who murdered her – he then committed suicide in that same well?"

"It was not suicide. But he too lies at the bottom of the well."

"And with them lies my great-great-grandmother's engagement ring, which was – stolen by ghosts?"

"Not by ghosts – it was stolen by something stranger and more dangerous than ghosts – something which remains an active and present danger up by bunk thirteen even today."

"Well, I've been rumored mad – but I should call you madder even than me," said Katie with the beginning of something like a smile, "were it not for that these past seven years I have lived things as mad as these you tell of every day."

As Katie said this I felt a tension break. Bryndis picked up her tea and said, "Sit down with us a while, Michael. Such a story needs a longer telling."

And so I sat, and told the story in full – everything Katrin had told me at the campfire of the dead, and all the horror of Julien Sorel and the spider-fox-faced web of darkness which followed after. At the end, I took out my Polaroid and we passed it around, each looking into the face of the long-dead girl above the fireplace, still much the same in a photo taken a mere two weeks before.

Of all the Morgans, surprisingly it was Bryndis who spoke first. "I cannot disbelieve you, Michael. I have been told before that Katrin Sigursson still walks the hills of Ketsanis with us – I was told by my mother, then by my niece Katie Eastman, and then by my daughter Katie here. Three Katies, all talking of a fourth. I think it is time I believed them." At this she looked at her daughter, as if asking for forgiveness.

Manly Morgan was silent for a moment longer, and then when he spoke it seemed to be mostly to himself that he was speaking. "I will wait until camp season is over," he said. "On the day after it is over I will have hired men come to cleanse the hillside of that place." I understood that he was referring to bunk thirteen. "I will have the well opened, its contents raised, the well itself filled in. The dead, if we find them, will be buried. The ring, if we find it, will be disposed of as Bryndis decides. May the dead then rest in peace," then looking at Katie, "and may the living go then in peace as well. Goodnight now, Mr. Chase; we thank you for what you have told us, but I have things to discuss with my wife."

"I will show him out," said Katie, "and perhaps ask a few questions on the way." She escorted me down the long hallway until we were once again in the Great Hall, from which I knew my way. She paused beneath the Sargent portrait, half visible in the dim light, and asked, "There is one thing I do not understand. Katrin has been dead these seventy years. Why were *you* chosen for this revelation, and why *now*?"

"I think it is just because he looked so much like me," I said. "When I saw him I was stunned; apart from his being shorter, Julien Sorel *was me*, as like as Katrin is to Bryndis in that portrait there. I think that fascinated and disturbed Katrin; she was willing to tell me her tale to be with me – and willing to see me die."

"Willing to see you die," echoed Katie. "You are right there. She is angry and she is cold, and has no pity for others, whose deaths she thinks much gentler than her own."

For the first time I felt that Katie was opening up to me, saying something that she might have just as easily kept to herself. It made me bold: "The note you left that night," I said, "it read 'let there be an end to Katie.' Everyone thinks you were referring to yourself. I do not think you were referring to yourself."

"You are right, I was not," confirmed Katie. "Nor was my grandmother when she wrote those words; nor was my cousin Eastman when she signed beneath them."

"So it is not news to you that Katrin Sigursson – lives?"

"Lives? She lives in me. She steals my life to live. I have felt her in me for maybe seven years. That her body lies at the bottom of a well is news. That she has been hungry for the life that was taken from her is not. She has taken me and used me and soiled me and I will no longer permit it, as my grandmother and cousin each found the strength one day to no longer permit it. Let there be an end to Katie – or let there be an end to me."

As she said this, I could feel a livid rush of anger surge through her. I was glad we were in half-light, for I do not think I would have wished to see her face at that moment. I changed the subject: "Did you know about that – thing – that web of darkness that might have killed me if you had not – I'm sorry -- distracted it?"

"That thing is named Ketsanis," she said, in a voice that was suddenly full of an inappropriate tranquility. "It is an old thing, and for many years it had no name, for naming is a human habit, and until it had taken humans into itself it felt no emptiness in lacking a name. But after it had consumed men it found itself hungry for a name, and it took for a name something its food often said before their deaths: 'Ketsa:nis.' It is Mohawk for 'I am afraid.' When my mother named this camp, the poor woman never knew she was naming it for fear."

As Katie spoke I had been growing tense with some nameless apprehension. Something had changed – I could feel it, but I did not know what it was. "I did not know your mother had named the camp," I said. "I thought it had been named by Eva Sigursson long ago."

"My mother named the camp," repeated Katie firmly, with the grimmest sort of smile. And then I understood. Instinctively, I glanced up at the portrait. Now Katie smiled more fully, and looked me in the eyes.

"I do not think you fully approve of me, my Julien," she said.

"I am not Julien," I said, "and you are not Katie Morgan."

"I am as much Katie Morgan as that accidental spirit who was gifted with this frisky body ever was," said – said Katrin. "I am as much Katie Morgan as I was Katie Astor, till my – shall I say, roommate? --   killed us both when I was not paying enough attention. I am as much Katie Morgan as I was Katie Eastman, until her mind broke in pieces and I had to let us die."

"Have you no mercy? You are inhumanly cold!" I said.

"All beauty – all superiority of any kind – is cold," she said, "and are we not all beautiful, all four of us?"

"But you are killing her!"

"And next it may be my pleasure to kill *you* again, my Julien. If the wolf regretted its kills there would be an end to wolves. Complain to the builders of the world if you find me remorseless."

"You were not remorseless in life," I said.

"And my virgin corpse wound up rotting at the bottom of a well for all my kindness; it was – it was quite the learning experience. Now I am as nature made me - I take what I want if I have the strength to take it. You are no different. First it was all 'kiss me kiss me Astrid' in bunk thirteen, now it's 'isn't Katie pretty, what would it be like to have her' – in front of her parents, no less."

"You have trespassed in my mind as well?" I asked in shock.

"You have been wrapped in the darkness of Ketsanis; there are no longer any secrets between us. Quiet your mind, and you will find that you can feel *us* as well; and already there are things inside us which you could not imagine which are feeding on you as you dream."

I was frightened. *Ketsa:nis.* I had thought the web of darkness which had threatened me had released me, but apparently all it touched remained within its grasp.

Katie saw my fear and relished it. "So you are lost, and now you know it. Come learn from me, take what you can of pleasure from that knowledge. There is no longer any virtue in being good. Do you want her?"

"I do not know what you mean."

"I am asking, do you *want* her? I mean, my lovely Katie, ready for your taking here in this half-darkness. I'll give her to you, if you want me to. I've lived a stolen lifetime as a woman; I could help young Katie do rough and tender things to you that she's hardly realized can be done yet. So what will it be, my second Julien? Will you be a wolf with me? Just tell me what you want - with hand and mouth and open thighs I will give it to you. Is this not a tempting body to do anything you've ever wanted with? All you need to do is to take what I am offering, without compassion or regret."

I wanted to slap her. Then with a laugh she was gone, and Katie – Katie Morgan -- pulled her arms to her chest and bowed her head in a burst of tears. I wanted to comfort her, to hug her, but I did not dare embrace her after what had gone before. She turned her tearful eyes up toward me again, and asked: "Now do you see why I must die?"

"Promise me, not yet," I said. "We are about to end all of this. When Katrin is at peace all of this will end. Please – promise me to wait."

But she said nothing, and ran from me back down the long hall to her own quarters. I did not know what to do – if I just left and later that night Katie killed herself I would hold myself to blame. I started back down the long hallway toward the Morgans' private rooms to alert her parents. But, halfway down the dark hallway, I ran into her running back toward me.

"I forgot to say – thank you," she said. "Thank you for holding her suggestions in contempt. And – I will not kill myself. I will help my father put Katrin in her grave. There will be an end to Katie – but not to me." With that she turned away, then turned back again, took my face in her hands and gave me a kiss. "This is Katie *Morgan* kissing you," she said, and was gone.

As I left the great Camphouse my mind was in a greater confusion than I had known since the night of the campfire of the dead. Katie Morgan and Katrin Sigursson were somehow aspects of the same person; one had kissed me, and the other had read me my death sentence – for I had been caught in Ketsanis's web. Although I had told my story, I still had that sense of some independent thing within me seeking expression; I still was plagued by that nagging sense of something I had forgotten, and suddenly I understood that if I ever came to remember, I would have to confront within myself something unwanted, foreign, and predatory – something hungry, which was not seeking to be released.

BONDYE

When I returned that night toward my bunk I was intercepted by Astrid, Chris, and Karen, who wanted to know how my story had been received by the Morgans. We retreated to the fire-ring between the lower six and the upper six bunks (the one above Bunk Thirteen being in use by a crowd of other counselors who had as yet been told nothing of my adventures). We did not light a fire – I told the story of my story by the moon and stars – everything but the last few minutes when Katie Morgan and I had been alone – I did not think Astrid needed to hear that part of the story.

"So Manly's known all along something's up with Bunk Thirteen," said Chris. "He's never said a word of it to anyone. And now that he knows just what's up, he'll have it torn down after this year's camp."

"Good riddance to it," said Karen. "But do you think that just giving those bones in the well a proper burial will stop the haunting?

Wasn't the place haunted before Julien Sorel or Katrin Sigursson ever got involved?"

"I think Manly's only thinking about his Katie," I said. "She's troubled by Katrin, possessed by her maybe if you accept that sort of thing – she's tried to kill herself to end it. I think Manly's all about: if Katrin is at peace in death, then Katie will be left in peace to live."

Astrid had been looking at me silently till then. "You seem upset," she said at last, taking my hand in hers, "but you haven't told us anything upsetting. Is there something you haven't told us?"

Perceptive Astrid – she had caught me. 'Well, … yes. When I was finished with her parents, Katie walked me to the door, and we stopped to talk by that painting of Katrin and Bryndis in the Great Hall. Then the … the Katrin Sigursson part of her spoke to me … and said I was not safe. Katrin says that spider-fox web-thing I saw by the campfire – which calls itself Ketsanis just like the camp – well, it didn't just leave me alone and safe when Mrs. Morgan screamed as I thought it did. Katrin says that it caught me in its web, and I could prove this to myself if I wanted because I should be able to feel what it's thinking as much as it can feel what I am thinking. And it can feed on me through that connection – whatever that means."

This reduced everyone to silence again. Chris and Karen stared uncomfortably at one another; Astrid pulled me close in a silent hug, but then spoke with decision. "So it will not be enough to bury Katrin Sigursson – we must destroy this Ketsanis."

"And how do we do *that*?" I asked, in something like despair.

"Can you really feel what it is thinking?" urged Astrid. "Then – what is *it* afraid of?"

"I do not know. I have not tried."

"Then try."

Everyone was quiet, waiting, so I closed my eyes -- and tried.

I felt nothing. I still felt that sense of something seeking expression within me, like a story that wanted telling, and that nagging sense of something I had forgotten -- but nothing more. So I worked with what I had. What was it I had forgotten? I felt around in my mind, as one does when one meets someone one has met before but struggles to recall their name. I felt around in my mind, but found nothing. So, I tried to put my mind aside, and think no thoughts, and let what would happen, happen.

At once I was passing through deep woods; the scent of fallen pine needles was all about me, and shafts of moonlight lit the forest floor where breaks in the canopy of pine overhead silhouetted tall trees against the stars. I was not walking so much as drifting. The mind in my mind was filled with music, piano music, passionate and tender, suffused with sorrow and regret – and indeed all of me, not just the music, was filled with sorrow and regret – and flashes of anger as well. Of anger – and as I felt the anger I was drawn into another realm of perceptions – equally passionate but vengeful, seeking redress against – everything. I was proud that I was clever and powerful, and I heard around me a clamor of things I had – humiliated – animal cries and the voices of men, but like a beast at hunt I was without mercy and took a cold joy in the clamor, for the clamor was my vengeance, and its inability to resist me demonstrated my power. My power – and as I felt the power, I suddenly saw a great light about me – or I *was* that great light for a moment, but it was too much to bear and at once I found myself grown small again, in a bed with the comfortable feel of sheets about me. I felt the warm embodiment of living human form again, but there was a great roaring of whispered words in my mind, and as I felt myself getting out of bed I felt in my hands a soft rag doll, which I could not see in the darkness but knew to be a young black girl with a great head of curly hair.

"Luigi!" I cried aloud. "I am holding Luigi's *Natra* doll!"

This was not anything Astrid, Chris, or Karen had been expecting to hear. Astrid could not manage anything more than a concerned "What?!"

"Katrin was right. I am connected to something when I quiet down my own thoughts. I felt myself moving through the forest – I was feeling what it was to be Katrin herself I think. Then I was, I think, Ketsanis – and I can tell you Ketsanis is not a friend to us. For a moment I was something – bigger - than Ketsanis, I do not know what it was … and then suddenly I was Luigi getting out of his bunk bed holding that little doll of his. But that's not good."

"Not good that Luigi's getting up?" asked Karen instinctively, thinking like a bunk counselor.

"No, not good for me to wind up feeling what it is to be Luigi – I think that means he must *also* be caught up in Ketsanis."

"Oh my god!" said Karen. "Chris, Astrid, you have to tell Mike what happened to Luigi today."

So they told me *their* adventure of the day. Ever since the "Luigi hurt" incident of a few weeks back, when Astrid had for a moment connected with Luigi, Astrid had been following Manly's advice and involving Luigi in the strenuous hikes of the upper-six campers, in the hope that this more arduous involvement with nature would again draw Luigi out of himself. But until today, nothing had happened. And what happened today was – different.

Astrid and Luigi had attached themselves to a bunk twelve hike led by Chris. They had done this before – the bunk twelve campers looked on Luigi as a sort of mascot and on the whole were either amused or unaffected by his tagging along. On today's hike Eddie Scrum, one of the twelvers, had slipped while scrambling over some rocks and been given much grief for this by his bunkmates, so he was not in a good mood by the end of their hike. Just as the group was returning down the old camp road into the hollow on the hillside where bunk thirteen and its fire-ring overlooked the valley below, Luigi, talking to his doll as usual, stumbled into Eddie and almost knocked Eddie down again.

"Watch where you're going, moron," said Eddie. He grabbed Luigi's doll out of his hands and threw it against a rock outcropping which marked the uphill side of the hollow, opposite the camp road from the fire-ring. Natra landed in a pool of clear rainwater which had gathered on the basin-like surface of a projecting chest-high rock.

Chris and Astrid were all over Eddie in a moment, but as before when Luigi had bobbled his doll into the ditch, Luigi unhesitatingly hurled himself toward the rock outcropping to retrieve his Natra. Chris said he moved faster than triathlete Astrid, and this time he did not hurt himself. Talking a rapid stream of word salad, he took his doll, now soaking wet, out of the standing water with his right hand and started slapping himself with his left on his cheek and upper chest, something he did when he was upset. Astrid started to gently restrain him, although he did not like to be touched at times like this. But as Luigi turned to try to free himself from Astrid he suddenly looked out toward the bunk twelve campers who had paused on the camp road watching this little drama play out, and beyond them to bunk thirteen, the fire-ring, and the valley beyond – and the expression on his face transformed. He squinted like he was staring into the sun and as his word salad trailed off into silence a big smile began to spread across his face. Everyone felt a great cooling of the air, as when a cloud passes over the sun on a chilly but sunny early spring day, and looked at one another as if to ask "did you feel that too?" Luigi slowly raised his dripping doll in front of him, as if offering it at some invisible altar, and said "Bondye!" to the empty air. Everyone was still for a moment – but then the moment passed and the chill was gone, and Luigi was bounding back toward the other campers saying "Bondye, Bondye, Bondye" to his Natra doll – and the incident was over.

I suppose at this point the four of us at the lower fire-ring would have started trying to tie this incident to my perception that Ketsanis had somehow caught Luigi, like me, in its web – but instead, Astrid suddenly stood up and took off toward the camp road. The other three of us looked, and saw a child-shaped mass of darkness against the lighter darkness of the moonlit night. Luigi was out of bed and walking up the road.

Astrid quickly intercepted him just below the upper six bunks and told him he needed to come back to bunk with her, but he paid her no attention, and evaded her gentle attempts to lead him with her hand on his back. He was looking up the camp road toward the upper bunks. I followed his gaze and in the distance saw another human-shape of darkness in the distance. Somehow I knew it was Julien.

"What do you see up there?" I asked.

Astrid, Karen, and Chris all looked up the road. "I see nothing," said Chris. The others all said the same.

"I see something," I said. "I think Luigi does too. I think it's the blind ghost."

"What do you see, Luigi?" asked Astrid. She did not expect a reply – Luigi did not respond to questions.

But this time, as if in response, he said, looking up the road: "Zonbi!"

"I would not let him go any further up the road," I said. "Keep him far away from bunk thirteen. We're safe way down here."

And then, as if to defy me, a woman's voice spoke quietly from the darkness, asking: "Louie?" Only Luigi and I heard it. It seemed to come from all around us. Luigi looked first one way then the other, eyes wide. "Manman?" he asked, "Manman? Manman?" as he turned from side to side in the darkness.

"I have heard this story before," I said to myself. "It's that fox thing being his mother. The same as with Julien a lifetime ago."

As I said this I looked back up the road at the dark shape I had taken for Julien, and startled. It was standing, its eyeless face pale as death in the moonlight, not ten feet up the road. I could feel its seething anguish radiating toward us. Astrid, Chris, and Karen seemed to see and feel – nothing. Whatever was going on, was apparently reserved for those Ketsanis had taken into itself. For us, proximity to that haunted hollow in which bunk thirteen had been built no longer mattered. Luigi looked back up the road, and once again said "Zonbi!"

At this, the image of Julien began to dissolve as before into a web of silvered darkness, as Luigi seemed to watch in fascination. "Anasi!" he said. I did not know what any of his Haitian words meant. I did not know what to do to protect us.

But then Luigi held up his doll before him, as I had been told he did earlier that day beside the rock outcropping up the hill, and between Luigi and the dark web of Ketsanis the moonlight seemed to gather itself into a shielding cloud of light, and Luigi cried out "Bondye! Bondye!" as I had been told he had done before. And with that all was over, and Luigi took Astrid by the hand and started to walk her back to bunk.

"Did you see *any* of that," I asked Chris and Karen, astonished.

"I sure did, but I don't believe it," responded Chris in amazement. "The autistic kid who doesn't like to be touched and doesn't know any of us exist took Astrid's hand and is leading *her* back to bunk. Manly will never believe this!"

Astrid was looking back over her shoulder at the three of us, grinning and shrugging, her hand tight in Luigi's.

None of them had seen *anything*. I had seen – but not understood.

CONVERSATIONS WITH THE DEAD

The next day, Chris and I told Manly of the previous night's incident on the old camp road. On the one hand, Manly was excited and amazed to hear of Luigi's taking Astrid by the hand, of his diminished word-salad, and of how a hard day's hike and a tussle with another camper had seemed to provoke Luigi's increased engagement with the world. On the other hand, the notion of Luigi's wandering off at night, of his – and my – connection with something dark in the forest that predated Bunk Thirteen, and above all, I suspect, his unspoken assumption that his own daughter might also be so connected – all these things filled him with a dread I am sure was greater than he would publicly acknowledge. He asked that day that Astrid and Luigi move into the Great Camphouse with his family, so he could see the changes in Luigi at first hand, and so he could be sure that they were safe. One of the activity counselors took Astrid's place as a bunk counselor, and Astrid became Luigi's personal trainer and therapist (which in Manly's view of therapy were, of course, much the same).

By that evening's meal, Katie Morgan had heard the whole story from her father. She pulled me aside during the meal, leaving stalwart Bummer to keep our campers focused on their meal without my help.

"So you are as screwed as I am," was her gentle introduction to the topic when we were alone. "You can feel her inside you?"

"Her? What her?"

"That slut my great-great aunt who ought to be dead in a well."

"It's not just her. It's Ketsanis. Maybe if Katrin finds peace you'll be fine. *Maybe*. But for me, and for that camper Luigi who's staying with you now, I need to find out how to get clear of the thing that killed Julien and Katrin in the first place. I think it also killed your great-great-grandfather, and that kid in bunk thirteen the first year of camp, and the people who dug that well under the bunk – I think it has been sucking at the minds of your family and God knows how many others for God knows how many years. It was not a small number I saw in its web around that campfire."

"So how do you propose to get clear of Ketsanis? The only way I thought of to escape Katrin was – not a pleasant option. My mother has kindly asked me if I would consider other alternatives next time."

"Astrid says I need to connect with Ketsanis inside myself and find out what it fears."

At the mention of Astrid a brief cold look came across Katie's face. Suddenly I was not very comfortable with the thought of Astrid and Katie sharing living quarters together. What would they say to one another when they were alone? But when Katie spoke, I became unsure whether that cold look had been meant for Astrid at all. "Yes, deepen that connection to Ketsanis, why don't you," she scoffed, "and then tell me what it's like when Ketsanis uses that same connection to explore *you*. Tell me of the groping as of cold hands inside your own heart and mind – *nothing* is shielded from it; tell me what it's like when you find yourself watching from a distance as your body goes about doing things you can no longer control. I've been there, Michael, and I know where that route ends." Here she took my hand and looked into my eyes, with a foreshadowing of tears in hers. "That is not a course I will let you take unwarned." Was she so concerned just because she saw in me an echo of herself? I looked into her lovely face out of a Romney painting, remembered her sudden kiss the night before, and wondered how many people one could be in love with at the same time.

"But how else am I to learn its weakness," I continued when I had re-collected myself.

"Katrin has been part of it for seventy years. Make *her* tell you. She thinks you look like the alpha version of her little Julien. She got you into this because she was fascinated by you. Make her tell you how to get out again - she owes you that much."

"But how could I do that if I do not make contact with her though Ketsanis, inside me – like I did last night? Will you let her communicate – through you?"

"Like hell, after that filthy show she put on for you to spite me. Never again, if I can help it. But you don't need to *become* her, or have me become her either. You just need to *ask* her. She told you she likes to walk the woods at night – and I can vouch it's true. You can find her in the woods – I will come with you. She's a showoff, she will not avoid us if we come to her together – her two *favorite* people! She will come to us, and we will make her give you what she owes you."

And so I went back to join Bummer with our kids, having an agreement to meet Katie after all my campers were asleep and go into the tall woods on the hill above the Camphouse, opposite to the hill on which the campers' bunks were built, where we would call upon Katrin and summon her from the darkness.

It was after nine PM that night when my kids were at last asleep and Bummer gave me the OK to go. I went down the hill and past the boathouse; I could see Katie sitting on the steps of the Great Camphouse in a Blondie T-shirt and jeans. She met me as I approached the Camphouse and led me around back. This was unfamiliar territory for me – family space, not camp space. We would not be bothered here by other counselors.

We followed a well-tended path up the hillside beyond the house, through an arboretum of planted trees that ended in cypresses and a small family graveyard. It was not spooky in the moonlight – merely peaceful. Katie pulled me aside off the path and indicated a large sculpture in marble of a woman, or rather a woman's body, laid out on an empire sofa under a veil. Beneath this were carved eight names with dates of birth and death, with space for two more as yet uncarved.

"Meet Bryndis and her children," said Katie. "Off behind her over there are Eva and Brownie, her parents, who were the first of us to live here. Do you see the same year of death for three of her children? That was the year of the Spanish Influenza. There are worse things in this world than Ketsanis."

"Is your grandmother buried here?"

"Just beside great-grandfather Astor there. And at the end is Katie Eastman's father, great-grandma Brynnie's youngest. Katie and her mother are buried beneath the cypresses over there."

"And the two empty places?"

"Brynnie always thought that Katrin had run off with her music teacher – that's what my family called Julien after he and Katrin were gone. She always thought that someday they would return. But of course, Brynnie died disappointed in this. She left it in her will, however, that two places would be reserved at her tombside for her dear sister and her dear sister's husband. And they are reserved still."

"Until in two weeks time, your father brings them back from the well and buries them here."

"That's the plan. It's a good thing the dead cannot choose their neighbors. As I read it, Ketsanis has one victim here – just Brownie. Katrin has two – my grandmother and cousin Katie. If my mom hadn't burst in on me a few weeks back, she would be at three, the equal of the great flu."

"I do not think she meant to kill. I think she just wanted a chance to live through all of you -- to live some of the life that had been taken from her."

"Our bodies were not hers to take. You do not think she meant to kill? Maybe not - but did she *mind* killing very much? I do not think so. But why should we guess – let's go ask her."

Katie took my arm and directed me back to the path. As the path continued into the woods beyond the graves, it became less well-maintained, and soon we found ourselves walking a simple forest trail through the great tall pines, until ahead of us moonlight shone through the canopy of branches on two small outcroppings of granite that almost cried out to be climbed on.

"This is a place where I am told Katrin and Brynnie played mermaids and pirates when they were little girls. This was the mermaids' rock, over there was the pirates'. If we wait for her here, I am sure she will come."

We grew silent and waited. Time passed. After a while, as had happened on the night of the campfire of the dead, I felt that tingle through the little hairs on the back of my neck which means "you are not alone." I looked at Katie. She nodded silently toward the pirates' rock. Beside the rock there was a deeper darkness forming than that of mere night, gathering itself in the shadow of the trees. When it saw it was observed, it stepped forward toward the edge of the moonlight around the rock. And there was Katrin.

She was not wearing her Gibson Girl attire from the painting, nor the nondescript frock of my Polaroid. Her hair was down, and she was wearing a white empire-style sleeveless dress, with low neckline and shoulders bare. I felt a surge of rage from the living Katie.

"You are wearing the ghost of my dress, great-great-aunt."

"It looks better on me. And after seventy years a girl grows bored with the same clothing, grand-daughter."

"You are not my grandmother!"

"I was there when your mother was born, it was I in command when she was conceived; it was I who cried with joy on the day that *you* were born. I am more your grandmother than ever was that weak accommodating girl who did not appreciate the gift of her own body. I lived longer as your grandmother than I did as – as *me* – until one day I was careless and lost control – and poor Katie was killed yet again, by her own hand."

I felt I had to step in between the two Katies before all this wound up in a place we didn't want to go.

"We have come to you for help," I said. "Help for the child Luigi. And – help for me."

Katrin looked at me, less coldly than before. Or perhaps I simply could not read the expression of her mostly-shadowed eyes.

"So my second Julien does not wish to be – consumed?" she said. "Neither did my first. Neither did I."

"But your death came too suddenly to avoid. Mine will not – Luigi's will not. We will go mad slowly - unless you help us. We need to find a way to make Ketsanis let us out of its web. We need to find what Ketsanis is afraid of."

"That's your girlfriend talking," said Katrin, and I felt another stab of anger from Katie. Katrin felt it too. "And I don't mean you, granddaughter," she said.

I had to redirect this before they started going at one another again. "You can help us learn what Ketsanis is afraid of, Katrin. You have been part of this for seventy years. Don't you want to be free too?"

At this I was sure I saw a change flit across Katrin's beautiful ghostly face in the shadows, but again I could not interpret it.

"Ketsanis does not fear," said Katrin. "Ketsanis *is* fear."

At this there was silence all around. Katrin shimmered in the darkness as if unsure whether to stay or go.

"So you will not help us," said Katie, surprisingly without anger or recrimination, in a tone of defeat. Katrin looked at her from the shadows.

"You know I did love you when you were born," said Katie. "I am not a beast. It just all ended too fast. Twice. Three times actually. I just wanted more. I am sorry. And – I *have* admired your strength. Even in death we can admire our adversaries, especially those whom once we loved."

Katie remained silent. She told me later she did not say anything because she was afraid that if she did she might cry.

Katrin then asked, although I can only guess why, "Will you love him?" and again there was silence. The two Katies were staring at one another. I felt very far away. "Very well," she continued, "I will give you your chance – even if for me it proves the end of chances."

Then addressing me, Katrin said "it is not to fear that you should look when fighting Ketsanis. The answer is before you in Luigi. Do you need my help to see it?"

"I do," I said. I felt Katie come back from whatever strange place her conversation with Katrin had taken her, and she grew attentive.

"Then it is time for me to tell you another story. Shall I summon up the image of another campfire on the rock?"

For a moment I almost imagined the warm glow of a fire burning in a hollow of the pirates' rock; I think it was a memory of Katrin's from very long ago. "I would like to hear your story," I said, "but this time I do not need the campfire."

So it was by the light of the moon on Pirates' rock that she told Katie and me a story that saved more lives than just ours.

"When he came to this camp, your little Luigi had a darkness about him. It was something that had grown from the absence of his mother and his anguish at her loss. To him it was a great darkness, though to Ketsanis it was small. It drew no notice from Ketsanis; like so many of the darknesses about your campers, it was not a rival, and it would not make much in the way of food.

"But then Luigi's doll was thrown into a pool of water in an outcropping of rocks, and Luigi reached into that water to retrieve it. Do you remember where that outcropping of rocks was, my second Julien? Do you remember how I told you of the spring of the Mohawks, which had long ago gone dry when the spirit of that place had grown offended by we over-proud Europeans? Well, that outcropping of rocks where Luigi's doll was thrown was the site of that old spring, and the water in that place, though merely the runoff of rainwater, was still sacred to the goddess. And when Luigi reached into that water, the goddess became aware of him.

"Now, you must see this as a goddess might see it. A young boy whose life and mind has been shattered, the prey of some corrupted darkness, in innocence reaches his hand into your waters. Here is no over-proud European bent on wresting from you your bounty and your secrets. Here is – a supplicant. Here is an opportunity for the giving of grace, which is what in your deepest being you as a goddess of nature have been formed at the beginning of time itself to give.

"So all at once the darkness is torn away from the child, and is consumed by Ketsanis as a greater spider consumes a lesser. Luigi is healing, and will continue to heal. You have told yourself Luigi has a connection to Ketsanis – yes, I have a connection to _you_, I have heard you think and say it. But you are not very observant, my second Julien! Like my first, you are blind. Luigi's connection is to the spirit of the spring, the spirit he calls Bondye, taking it for the great spirit of the Haitians.

"Now the spirit of the spring, as I have told you before, has in its anger become corrupted and caught in the web of Ketsanis, and so it seemed to you that Luigi's connection was to Ketsanis. But Ketsanis and – Bondye – are not the same, and the spirit of the spring's helping Luigi, who to Ketsanis is no more than meager food, has driven something of a wedge between them. And it is this, not fear, which is your opportunity."

I heard all this, but I did not hear. I understood that Luigi's connection was not directly to Ketsanis, but to a spirit itself caught in Ketsanis's web, but I did not understand how this was an opportunity for me. Katrin seemed to hear my confusion, and so continued.

"Do you need me to be more clear? Then I will be more clear.

"Long ago, as I have told you before, the death of something so small as a spider tore a hole in the fabric of the world, as so many holes are torn each and every day. This happens all throughout creation – the world is torn, and the world is healed again. But sometimes the healing proves slow, when anger and the lust for vengeance are not put aside, and this case of the spider proved one of the slow cases. The absence – or shall I say, the ghost - of the spider resonated with anguish and pain, it hungered for vengeance, and into it were drawn the Blue-Jay chicks to which the spider had been fed, and then their fierce mother, along with the snake that had eaten all of them, and the weasel that ate the snake, the wolf that ate the weasel, and so on through the whole succession of murder and pain which is everyday life in the quiet of these great woods. All who were caught in the growing web of darkness woven by the absence of that spider were consumed.

"For unnumbered years it dwelt near here, a dark spot in the dark forest which living creatures learned to avoid. As it grew isolated its hunger grew, and as it moved about in search of fresh life to consume it came across a thing far greater than itself, a spirit from the days when even greater things had visited from worlds which have no name and made this land, a spirit at play in the waters of a spring she protected on the hillside.

"The thing that had started as the ghost of a spider caught her in its web, though she was a greater thing than it, and for a while it was not clear whether she would grow cruel, or the spider-thing would grow kind. Such was the state of affairs when the Mohawks knew and honored our Goddess as a spirit generous to the humble and death-dealing to the proud, though they knew nothing of who she was beyond that she was guardian of a spring along their path to the high mountains. But when she was raped and weakened by later men the balance shifted in the spider's favor, and the goddess in her web grew dark with anger, and became a thing of vengeance, and seemed to lose her memory of when she had been a thing of light.

"You startled when I said the goddess was raped – but I did not choose that word without cause. I have told you how when she felt insulted she withdrew her waters from the land, but then men came to take what they were not given, and tore that hole we call a well but she calls a wound in her hillside, to seize with violence what she would not give. There are many wrongs done in the world, and many of these we learn to forgive, but rape is not one of them. Not for a woman, still less for a goddess.

"And so the light of this spirit became dark with a lust for vengeance. The spider taught her malice and a fox which had perished miserably in her wound taught her craft. And then - so many of us became their food! Most have lost all form and individuality, and are no more than knots of darkness in a web. My father is in here, but has already been consumed past speech or recognition. My Julien is here, but he is destroyed, destroyed utterly and is no longer human. I am in here, and I am still somewhat of who I was, for by keeping me this way the cruelty of which I am a part can continue to feed on me - on my longing for all I have lost. But as time passes I will grow darker, and become just another density in the web.

"You – you who look so like Julien – you have awakened me, but at first only to cruelty. I would have been content to watch you die. Or, to hold you against me, kiss your lips, feel your arousal and remember what it was to be alive. But all that shall pass, and is already passing; you and I shall become empty shells in the web of darkness - unless I give you to my silent Katie there, teach you to tear apart Ketsanis, and then be torn myself from its anguished energy and become – nothing at all.

She must have heard me think *what do you mean – tear apart Ketsanis?* for she paused in her flow of words and redirected her attention toward me.

"Did you like the sound of that, my second Julien? Are you so quick to end my voice, to have me become nothing? Well then – perhaps so am I. So let me tell you this: why would a goddess who has been party to the creation of these mountains and these woods wish to go through eternity as a spiderfox god of vengeance and darkness? If she were healed, made whole, might she not tear the very web of darkness which confines her and make herself free? I do not know if the spiderfox would be diminished or destroyed – but I do not think the makers meant such things as it to be a part of their building, and I do know that the goddess caught in this web is a far greater thing than the web itself. That is the lesson of your Luigi – inside the darkness, the goddess is still a spirit who yearns to bring grace and healing, not vengeance and destruction. Give her the opportunity to be who she was meant to be, and she will burst forth in joy, and Ketsanis will be destroyed – and that is the way to salvation you have asked me to tell you.

"The fabric of the world is often torn, but I believe it always heals. Yet, in its healing the world will be rid -- of me. With Ketsanis gone, I will not have the energy to remain. I was pretty Katie, happy Katie, so very long ago – then I was killed, and more than my life was taken from me, for I have become a food of darkness and a darkness myself, and when the world is healed it will be rid of me."

I interrupted Katrin there. "I do not think you will just cease to be," I said. "I think you will be free to – to journey on. I do not know to where."

"There is no 'me' to go on that journey without destination," she responded. "I am not Katrin Sigursson. I am an absence where she used to be. Maybe *she* has moved on, *I* do not know. But I don't think I am her. I am nothing. I think that is why I have been cruel - I thought it would make me *feel*. But I think all I am is a cold and empty hole. If Ketsanis is broken, I shall just cease to be. But, tonight, I have accepted that."

"You are not a cold and empty hole," said Katie Morgan, breaking a long silence. "The well where you were murdered is, but you are not. You are – better than I had thought you. I remember again those first years when I felt you about me – how much I loved you then. You hurt me afterwards – but I think I begin to understand you – and if it matters to you for me to say it, I do forgive you," she concluded, then added with a smile, "even if you have stolen my dress."

The Katies were looking only at one another; I knew I was forgotten. "Good bye, now, Katie Morgan," said Katrin, "daughter of my bright-eyed baby Bryndis, granddaughter of poor Katie Astor, great-granddaughter of my long-gone Brynnie – all of whom I have loved, and some of whom I have *been*. Perhaps the makers of the world will yet allow us to try again from fresh beginnings, someday, you and I, if such things may be permitted. But of such things, who can say? Now, go do what you must do."

And then she was gone.

Hand in hand, trembling in a stunned silence, Katie and I walked together out from the moonlight-spackled woods to the camp in the valley below. We chastely kissed good-night.

I did not go directly back to my bunk however. I walked past all the lower six, and the upper six as well. I stood before bunk thirteen in the moonlight. I heard the rattling of branches above, the grating of stone over stone within. In the darkness I heard the whisper of unintelligible voices. But I did not give a damn. I walked past the bunk, to the outcropping of rocks just where the camp road rose from the hollow around bunk thirteen on its way to the woods beyond. I found a projecting stone with a basin-like surface around chest height in which the runoff of recent rains had pooled. I placed my right hand into the water and spoke aloud:

"I do not come in pride," I said. "I do not ask to command the power of this land or learn the secrets of its dead. I come only to tell you this, great goddess of gentle waters: give me but two weeks and this well which has offended you will be filled in. If this gash cut in your hillside has been an offence to you, then in honor and respect this offence will be ended. And – we thank you for your kindness to the little Haitian boy whom you are healing. May we who have done wrong to you now treat you with the kindness you have shown to us unasked and without reward."

The temperature about me plunged. I heard a resonance in the air form itself into speech, quietly commanding "Heal my wound," using Katrin Sigursson's voice. There was no fear or threat in it. My offer had been accepted.

As I walked back from the rocks there was nothing but silence from bunk thirteen. Whatever dwelt in there was quiet, watchful – and, perhaps, surprised. Back in my bunk, I lay awake looking at the bottom of the bed above me. I tried to quiet my mind. In the stillness I felt that familiar sense of something seeking expression within me, which I knew now to be my connection to Ketsanis. I did not try to open that doorway to what Ketsanis was experiencing, as I had done with Astrid, Chris, and Karen the night before, but from standing just outside that doorway, as it were, I could feel something of a great tumult going on within. And what I felt was something like anger and something like shock, but even more it felt like – fear.

With a quiet sense of victory I passed at last into sleep.

ONCE MORE UNTO THE BREACH

The last two weeks of camp passed without event – or perhaps it was that my mind was occupied, awaiting the cleansing of Bunk Thirteen, and what other events there were paled into insignificance. Luigi did continue to improve, interacting with Astrid even when not hurt through hiking misadventures or threatened by occult forces. And, Astrid did cut me loose in the lightest of ways one evening. A day or two after Katie and I had our interview with Katrin Sigursson, Astrid came up to me after dinner as we were herding our kids back toward their bunks, gave me a quick kiss on the cheek, and said "don't worry about me, counselor, you're not the only cute guy in camp." And then she was off - had she just broken up with me? I was only sure of it when Katie Morgan began to be much more comfortable being – affectionate – with me that evening. Neither of them have ever admitted it, but I am sure that Katie and Astrid, together one evening in the family quarters of the Great Camphouse, had sat down together and sorted out my life for me. How deeply strange is this, our world, when we look into its dark places! For we who would get on with the business of being men, with homes to maintain and gardens to tend and illusions of security to preserve, perhaps it is best there are things discussed between women we can never know and stories of how men's lives are arranged that we will never be told.

At last, the final day of camp arrived. Everyone said their goodbyes; the aggressive campers feigned indifference while the passive ones grew suddenly emotional. Chris and Karen went off to say their end-of-summer goodbyes to one another – they both had other commitments and neither was staying for the cleansing of bunk thirteen next day. Astrid, Luigi, and I were staying on with the Morgans to accomplish the end of things. The camp without its campers seemed strangely deserted; it may be that the extremity of death is not required for absences to form and take possession of newly-quiet spaces once the hectic press of life has departed from them. Toward evening, a truck drove up the old camp road to bunk thirteen – it left a load of earth which was meant for filling in the well the next day. That night, Bryndis Morgan took out a Parcheesi board and we all played; somehow, no one wanted to talk of tomorrow. Even Luigi held his *Natra* doll in one hand and Astrid's hand in the other, and was still.

In the early morning, not long after a quiet breakfast, three more trucks arrived at camp: first a group of men who would demolish the bunk and cart away its remains, then a well repair firm which had been hired to accomplish the removal of the bones, and finally a group of laborers who would fill in the well with the earth which had arrived the previous night. A policeman who had something to do with observing the removal of the bones also arrived and went up the hill with Manly. The three trucks followed behind, and the cleansing of bunk thirteen began.

By mid-morning, when Astrid, Luigi, Katie, and I went up the hill, all remains of the wooden structure were gone; only the now-exposed well remained. At a distance, I immediately heard the rattling of dead branches in the air above where the bunk had been, as well as a group of Jay chicks calling for their mother. Julian Sorel seventy-three years before had heard the same, and wondered at the seemingly causeless rattling of branches. I had the advantage of sight, and saw not only that there were no moving branches nearby which could cause such a rattle, but that there also was no birds nest anywhere nearby from which Jay chicks could be calling. *None of this is real*, I said to myself, *this too is something from long ago, from the death of a spider in the forest when the woods were young.*

The men who had demolished and removed the bunk had already gone on their way, and the well repair crew had erected some sort of scaffolding around the well, with a harness which could hold a man and a large bucket deeper than it was wide, both of which could be lowered into the darkness of the well. But the well-cap stone was still in place, and as I and my companions approached we heard above the rattle of long-dead branches and the cries of long-dead birds a sound of stone grinding over stone and men's voices in argument.

The well-cap stone was nervously shifting, several inches at a jerk, from side to side. The workers had withdrawn to a distance and were telling Manly that they would have nothing more to do with this job. It was only the force of Manly's personality which still kept them at the site – or perhaps it was the dilemma that they could not abandon their equipment, but nor could they retrieve it without approaching what they now believed was a cursed or haunted well.

"You can all go to hell," I heard Manly's voice say. "I'll deal with this myself. Get out of here!"

At this, a few of the workers began to gratefully head for their truck, but several others, the policeman, and Manly himself stood rooted to where they stood. Manly himself knew that *he had not said this*. The workers who had been looking right at Manly knew the same, and did not know what to make of it. I could feel that things were about to get bad.

Astrid took command of the situation in her usual confident way. She took Luigi by the hand and walked right up to the well. She beamed at all the big men trembling. "You people are so easily spooked!" she said. "Yeah, the well's haunted. Why do you think we're filling it in? But it can't hurt you. It groans, rolls that stone around, there are voices … *so what?* I've heard all this before; I'm not afraid of it, my little friend Luigi here is not afraid of it – are *you* afraid of it?"

Manly took advantage of the moment. "Let's get rid of that stone," he said, and looked several of the largest workers one by one in their eyes. They followed him. The stone began to slide itself around violently. "At my count!" said Manly. "One push and it's off."

He and two other men put their hands on one side of it, like séance participants with their hands on a quivering Ouija planchette. "One – two – THREE!" and with a single push the large stone crashed to the far side of the well, and the darkness of the well-shaft was exposed to the sun – and to the well cleansing apparatus, all prepared for its descent.

The slender man who had originally expected to be lowered into the well to retrieve Katrin and Julien's bones had no intention of being lowered into a haunted well, but still he stepped forward toward his larger companions and Manly to look down the shaft of the well, as did the policeman. They all suddenly jerked back in horror.

It had been like looking into the mouth of the lair of a trapdoor spider – black filaments of night wound tight against the walls and halfway down gathered in the center as a darkness which sealed the well. Looking into it the men had seen the darkness change form, a silvery night within it taking the shape of something like a fox's face, angry and cornered, with teeth bared, but with stalks like those of a great repulsive spider for eyes. As the men jerked back, Luigi cried out "Anasi!" and more closely squeezed Astrid's hand.

It was immediately clear that no one from the well repair firm would be descending into the Morgans' well that day. The cop said "Just fill it in!" and the workers immediately nodded in agreement.

To look at Manly was to know that what he was experiencing here was past his worst imaginings. He understood that the thing he had seen in the well was the Ketsanis I had described to him, and that it was protecting itself by preventing the cleansing of the well. But Matthew Morgan knew of only one way to deal with fear, and that was to crush it. No sooner had the policeman given his order to fill in the well than Manly said, in his firmest and most commanding voice, "That will leave two bodies imprisoned down there − and my daughter will know no peace. Leave it to me then. I'm going down."

"No. Let *me* go down," I heard myself saying. "I am a bit smaller, it will be easier for me."

Manly looked at me hard. I continued: "I am also unwilling for this to go on any longer. I also will not permit Katie - or anyone else - to continue to suffer."

Manly seemed to be wrestling with a decision. I think he thought it would be cowardly for him to let anyone other than himself go down into the horror he had seen in that well. But at the same time, I think he doubted that any of his workers would have the courage to stay with us for more than a moment once he was out of sight down the well. He gave me a nod, and I understood. It was to be me.

I walked to the edge of the well and looked down. Whatever everyone had seen in there before was gone, or had hidden itself. Manly and Katie came up beside me.

"Can't we just lower some claw down there and pull the bones out?" he asked. But we all knew in our hearts that we needed to provoke in Ketsanis a war with itself, and this would not be achieved through passivity or cowardice. Katie began to say something to me, but the words died on her lips. She later told me she had meant to say I did not need to do this for her − but as she began to speak she understood that this needed doing for others as well, and she lapsed

59

into silence. She felt what we were all, I think, feeling: I needed to goad the spider-fox that wanted us dead to a rash attack against myself, the man who had pledged healing service to the Goddess, so as to bring the Goddess to our aid and thus tear whatever Ketsanis had grown to be asunder. And to do this – *I* had to go down the well.

So I was strapped into the harness and the workers found the bravery if not to go down the well themselves then at least to stand beside the well and work the apparatus. I swung out into the space above the well-shaft and the ropes tautened. And then I felt my lowering begin.

Unlike Julien so many years before me I was not blind, and the decent into the well was a descent into darkness. Perhaps also because I was not climbing down under my own power, I had more leisure than he had for fear. In the silence of the well I imagined the whispering of voices, angry unintelligible voices and the threatening growling of cornered animals in the air about my ears. I tried not to listen - and then was suddenly startled when I felt my feet hit something. There were indeed bones down here; as I was lowered the last few feet I had to brush aside a clear space for myself with my feet.

I was at the bottom. Soon the bucket would be lowered and I would scoop the bones into it. After a few minutes I would be done and gone. But then there was a silvering of the darkness around me, and I saw I was not alone. With a blast of cold, the spider-fox was forming in the darkness of the well beside me. It mocked me in Katrin's words and voice: *See, see what you have done to me*, turning up its curled fox lips and fixing me with its spidery stalked eyes. Above me Manly was calling my name. I could escape by crying for help but had no power. Like Julien I understood: I could die down here. But Ketsanis did not reach out to freeze my heart, and Manly did not wait for my cry; taking my silence for trouble he had me pulled out. As I was rapidly pulled free, I felt the 'thing' in the well with me in a state of maximum tension. I said to myself: *the goddess wants to be healed, but the spider-fox wants to catch us all in its web.*

When I reached the surface I was exhausted - but alive. I had accomplished nothing – save not being killed. But I quickly realized that few eyes were on me. On the ground beside the well, Katie lay in a sort of convulsion. Whatever tension I had felt in Ketsanis was in her as well. Astrid was holding Katie's head in her lap, and Katie was rolling her eyes and speaking in voices, angry unintelligible voices and the growls of animals, just as I had heard in the well.

And truth to tell, the tension was in me too. I could barely free myself from the harness and fall on the ground beside Katie. The roaring in my head was enormous. That weeks-old sense of something seeking expression within me was resolving itself as a dozen voices in my head, all crying out in synchrony with the voices emerging from Katie's lips. There was such a roar of sound! Voices within and without, overhead the cracking of branches as of winter forests in a gale, the cries of angry birds like harbingers of death, it was all too much, too much …

Around me, the workers and the cop seemed frozen less in fear than in amazement. Manly from beside the well looked down on his daughter thrashing in Astrid's arms and understood: my daughter will die. Maybe now, or, if we back off, then maybe later – but this thing intends to kill her, and it will. He looked down into the darkness of the well.

"Fuck it," he said. "Strap me in. I'm going down."

Somehow his tone of command was such that despite the poster child for possession that was Katie, the workers, as if in battle, obeyed. Down he went, and, to the degree he could later remember it, all was quiet as he descended, as it had been for me. Even before he reached bottom, he called for the basket to be lowered. As he reached the bottom he stood in the space I had made and waited for the basket to reach him. He felt a sudden soft thump of something wet on his head and heard it land in the bones beside him. He reached down, and picked up Luigi's soft rag doll. It was soaking wet.

Above him, and unknown to all of us while Astrid was tending to Katie, Luigi must have retreated from the well side to the rock outcropping on the hillside where his doll had once been thrown, and then come back to the well side again to throw his *Natra* doll down into the darkness, all soaked with water from the basin-like rock at the outcropping. Through the roaring of voices in my ears I heard him crying "Bondye! Bondye! Bondye!" at the well side.

And down below, as Manly heard these cries, he felt a piercing cold about him, and saw a silvering of the darkness. He had never seen Ketsanis up close before. It was a loathsome thing to see form before you, not a foot away in the darkness of the well. He heard it mock him in his wife Bryndis's voice – some phrase he would never tell me that was special to the two of them. He saw it assume a grotesque parody of Bryndis's face, but with the sharp teeth of a fox and the stalked eyes of a spider. He felt it reach a paw of icy darkness through the little doll he was holding as if in protection before him toward his chest, toward his rapidly beating heart. Like Julien and like me before him, he suddenly had to confront what it was to die. And he found: he was willing to die, if it was needed to heal his daughter – but if she could not be healed? Well then he could accept death as well, if only because he would not then want to live. All he asked for was her healing.

And in that moment, holding the dripping doll close to his chest now as if he were a child – a child preparing to die – in that moment there came a great tearing shriek through all the fabric of the air, and the silvery thing of darkness before him was torn apart like the smoke of a leaf-fire at evening, torn as if by a great wind to reveal tall birch-like trees with fernlike flowers, a forest scene from the dawn of forests, as much greater mountains than any he had ever seen stood mighty in the distance and a great torrent rushing from their icy slopes passed beside him and splashed him laughingly in its waters.

Manly was stunned by the brilliance of this sudden vision and he must for a brief moment have passed out – or at least lost all sense of individual identity. When he came to, the bucket had been lowered beside him and voices were calling to him from above. "Do not lift me out!" he cried, with what strength he could muster. "I am OK, let me finish my work!"

Manly reached out in the darkness and began lifting bones into the bucket. It was long slow work, and several times he needed to have the bucket emptied to continue. Among the bones were two skulls, and below one of them was a ring. He pocketed the ring and called to be lifted out of the well.

At the surface the roaring of voices in my head had ceased, as had the crisis taking place inside Katie. We were both exhausted – but free. There was no rattling of branches, no crying of birds, no trembling of the well-cap stone. Manly gave the *Natra* doll back to Luigi, and looked out at the policeman standing by the bones, and the workers standing around the well like survivors after a battle.

"And what are all of *you* waiting for?" he boomed, as if nothing at all had happened. "Fill it in!"

THE END OF KATIE

It was several hours before the well was fully filled and the workmen headed down the hill to begin telling stories which they knew would never be believed. Shortly after the filling of the well commenced, the policeman had gone down the hill with Manly, who was much more weakened by his experience in the well than he was prepared to admit. Manly wanted to update Bryndis on everything, as she had been too ill and too nervous about the day's doings to join the party by the well. They would then prepare for a small burial service to be held that evening in the family graveyard out behind the Camphouse – the interment of Katrin Sigursson and Julien Sorel in the plots reserved for them by Katrin's long-dead sister.

Katie, Astrid, Luigi and I stayed behind to see the well filled in. We wanted to see this thing to its end. But after almost an hour Luigi began to grow restless, so Astrid said good bye to us and took him back to the Camphouse.

After the workmen had gone, Katie and I were left alone on the hill, sitting on the logs of the fire-ring in silence. Around us, the soundscape of the hillside told the stories of the lake and settled valley below, mixed with the the stories of the deep woods above, as it had in Julien and Katrin's day. There was a sound of digging from below – the digging of a double grave – and water was lapping on boats which had not yet been brought into the boathouse with the end of summer. Somewhere in the woods there was a gentle stirring of wind through the treetops, and a scamper of squirrels through the branches. And in all that soundscape there was no anomaly, no threat.

Katie looked at me after a while. "Is it time to go now?" she asked.

I hesitated. I was not ready to go yet. At first Katie seemed puzzled, but then a look of understanding came over her face, as if to say *you do not need to answer, I think I understand.* She kissed me without a word and began to go down the hillside. But then with a mischievous look she turned to me and said: "You love her for her beautiful ghost – those green eyes even now have lost none of their power. But remember – she has been dead since before your grandmother was born. Her face, her eyes: just memories, lovely memories of a beauty that is long gone." And then, after a pause: "When you are ready, you will find me waiting in *this* world, down below."

And indeed Katie was correct. I stayed - because I felt Katrin about somewhere, and I wanted to say goodbye.

I stood up from the fire-ring and walked over to the lower stretch of the hollow, where bunk thirteen had been. All was gone now, well and all. I walked back to a sunny grassy spot on the far side of the old camp road, near the stone outcropping where Luigi had dampened his Natra for Manly in the waters of a goddess. I lay down in the grass and closed my eyes and felt for Katrin. When I opened my eyes again she was reclining on one arm on the grass beside me, with her hair down, still wearing the ghost of Katie Morgan's white dress.

She reached out to take my hand – but already there was no ghostly chill, no tingle: I could feel nothing of her. She looked over at me and, smiling, asked: "Now - let there be an end to Katie?"

I wanted to squeeze her hand, but there was no substance there to squeeze. All I could do was look into her eyes and say "No. But perhaps at last it is time for Katie's journey."

This seemed to touch her. I sat up; she leaned back into the grass, and looked into the far distance. "Already I am almost gone," she said. "Soon I will learn if there is anywhere I am going."

She paused, then turning the perfection of her eyes back from the distance to look into mine for the last time, with her final words she suggested one last boundary to try to cross together: "Perhaps you can come a little of the way with me? I must say good-bye now, but perhaps there is still enough of Ketsanis in us both that you may stay with me a little after I am gone?" And with this she passed from my sight forever. I thought she meant I should stay a little while at this place where we had parted. But as I closed my eyes with the beginning of tears, I *did* still feel her presence about me; some of what she must be still experiencing was linked to me and present in my mind as well.

There was a dark sky about her, and in it a single sharp bright star. As she looked at it, it seemed to grow brighter still -- until as it grew almost too bright to bear it rose swiftly into a distance that opened overhead before her. As her eyes followed it they seemed to close softly over the star -- and that was the end of all seeing. But in that moment I believe there also came to her some revelation that was past my ability to experience, for I felt a surge of awe, and at once I felt set free in a universe composed of – so many! And with no separation at all between her aloneness and that great many, she was at peace with, and at *play* with, all the world.

With that all communion ended, and my mind was mine alone. As I sat with an almost painful pressure of tears against my closed eyes in silence, I suddenly realized my hand on the ground was wet, and opened my eyes. For a moment the grass all about me seemed to sparkle with dew, as if the earth itself had also shed tears for Katrin. But then, with an even greater wonder, I realized that this damp was more than dew or rain; from the rocks on the hillside above the hollow where bunk thirteen had been, water was flowing beside and around the little patch of grass on which I was sitting and running down the hillside. The spring of the Mohawks was flowing! As my tears fell free and gratitude swelled deep within me I splashed the water on my arms, on my face, and all about me, giving thanks to the free spirit that had once been caught within Ketsanis, giving praise to all there is that brings redemption unforeseen, and offering a tribute of laughter and tears to our unknowable world itself, which though dangerous and strange past all imagining I understood at last to be in its deepest nature generous, and not unkind.

And that was the End of Katie.

So I have come to the end of my tales of Bunk Thirteen. What more would you like to know? That Luigi is healed? That Katie Morgan and I are married now? That Matthew Morgan makes a most forbidding father-in-law? We still run our summer home as a camp for troubled children, but its name is no longer Ketsanis, as it is no longer a place of fear. We are Camp Ohneka now -- the *Camp of the Waters* -- a name we have taken to honor the spirit of the Mohawk Spring and of this generous land itself, which is not ours, though we are fortunate to be its guardians. If our summer home is growing year by year in its reputation as a place of help and healing for troubled children, I can credit the restorative of outdoor living and the enthusiasm of our counselors, but would add: it helps immensely to have a beneficent goddess as your silent partner.

It was two years ago that my Katie took her great-great-grandmother's engagement ring as her own, and four months ago that our precious young Katrin was born, another beauty in the Sigursson tradition, with the faintest of suggestive birthmarks on her neck, and a love of music already evident when she hears her mother sing. We have also had our troubles, as all in this world must, and it is lonelier here with Bryndis gone. But all our pain is borne with patience and our joy each day renewed when Katie and I hold Katrin in our arms, and look with hope into her newborn fresh green eyes.

ABOUT THE AUTHOR

Michael A M Coleman, having reached his 50s somehow while he was not paying attention, has passed unobtrusively through Harvard, the University of Chicago, and both halves of the House of Morgan, and now lives a quiet private life with his lifelove Pam and a dwindling number of dogs in North Stamford, Connecticut. His poetry collection *To Love and To Create* is published by Alabaster Leaves Publishing, an imprint of Kelsay Books.

www.ingramcontent.com/pod-product-compliance
Lightning Source LLC
Chambersburg PA
CBHW071345130626
46556CB00005B/2043